Awaken
stories from the
otherside

Aaron Barron

ISBN (E-Book): 979-8-9858394-0-1
ISBN (Paperback): 979-8-9858394-2-5
ISBN (Hardcover): 979-8-9858394-1-8
First Print Edition- March 2022

Published by Cosmic Innovations, LLC
Email: aaronbarronwrites@gmail.com

Dedicated to my family:
My mom, Rosolynn, for all your guidance and feedback.
My brothers, Ahmad and Ashton, for your unique perspectives.
My dad, Niquel, for giving me the courage to be myself. These are all the stories I know you'd love.

Acknowledgements

This wouldn't be possible without the work of great individuals that are behind me. Thank you all sincerely for reading my stories, providing critique, and simply listening.

Contributors: Rosolynn Barron, Laura Jones, Nahlah Abdur-Rahman, Ahmad Abdur-Rahman, Benjamin Williams, Sade Dozan, Maya Pete, Maya Thompson
Copyeditor: Francesca Singer
Formatter: Rosemary Aboh
Proofreader: Rose Fall
Book Design Illustrator: Jori Tytus

Contents

CHAPTER ZERO

A VOICE EMERGES FROM THE ETHER.

STORIES ARE OUR GREATEST GIFT TO THE WORLD. AS WE PROGRESS THROUGH THIS LIFE, WE COLLECT EVER-RADIANT SOUVENIRS IN THE FORM OF MEMORIES. MAY THESE MEMORIES OVERFLOW INSIDE OUR MINDS TO CREATE A CONSTELLATION. WE PLAY AMONGST OUR STARS IN TIMES OF UNCERTAINTY, CHERISHING THEM IN OUR DARKEST MOMENTS.

THERE ARE ELEMENTAL FORCES THAT COMPOSE THE COSMOS. MUSICAL SCALES ARE WEIGHED IN THE BALANCE AS OUR UNIVERSE PLAYS AN EVERGREEN SYMPHONY. MANY NAMES CAN BE ATTRIBUTED TO THESE FORCES, BUT THE ULTIMATE TWO ARE LOVE AND FEAR.

BEYOND THIS REALM EXISTS A WORLD INHABITED BY LOVE. THE ONLY WAY TO COMMUNICATE TO THIS REALM IS THROUGH WILLING VESSELS. THIS BOOK IS ONE SUCH VESSEL. BEFORE YOU ARE THE STORIES FROM THE OTHERSIDE.

AWAKEN.

Deja Vu

Chapter One

A chime goes off as the elderly man enters the kitchen. An eruption of joyful noise from the other room overflows into the otherwise peaceful setting. He shuts the door, putting a single finger over his mouth. *Shhhh.* He dusts off the confetti on his shoulders and walks over to the nearest counter to pour himself a drink. He sees enough Vodka for a small town but keeps looking around. Eventually, he finds his desire: an unopened bottle of scotch whiskey. Smiling to himself, he applies a heavy pour in his glass and sits down at the countertop.

A brown leather fedora covers the bald spot on his head. He's a well-dressed individual, wearing a navy-blue blazer on-top of a white tee. He rocks a silver necklace and platinum watch on his right arm. Business casual with subtle flair has always been his preferred outlook of life; not to mention, this is a special occasion. He checks his watch—a redundant habit—and chooses to take a sip.

At that moment, a hearty figure enters from the same door. Stumbling in as she enters, she exclaims,

"Whew, it's too bright in here."

She sees the man holding the drink, and pouts.

"Starting without me?"

"You're late," he responds, staring right at her with mild amusement. She's stout, rocking an afro straight out of *Foxy Brown*. Jewelry adorns every inch of her body: rings on each finger with a different horoscope sign emblem; two gold necklaces with the sun and crescent moon, respectively; dazzling rose-gold hoops hang from her crown. She has all the makings of a Queen, with none of the regality.

She cackles. "Wouldn't you know? No, you're right, okay, my bad," she explains, grabbing the whiskey bottle. "I was coming from light-years away, there weren't many starships headed to this galaxy. I had to hitch a ride from a meteor, if you can believe it."

She pauses, glancing at him, "What are you going by?"

He straightens up on his stool. "Ajala."

"Ah, how precise. Nice to meet you, Ajala. I'm Shoha."

"Ha. Indeed, you are." He raises up his glass, and she, her bottle.

"To new endings. Happy New Year," he says. She smirks, and plops down on the accompanying stool.

"So, are you going to tell me why you're an old man? I mean, what's up with that?"

"It fits my character," he responds succinctly.

"Not much of a talker? This should be fun."

"What about you, though?" he asks. "Where did you find this beautiful woman?"

"She is from Melbourne, Florida. Her name is Julia. Really great style, smart too. You know how rare that is for a human?"

He nods. "All too well."

"So. What are we supposed to be doing?" she asks, twiddling her thumbs.

"I have no idea," he responds. He's still in awe that such a thing is happening. This feeling of uncertainty hasn't existed in him for some time, and yet he welcomes the newness of it all. Just then, he snaps his fingers.

"Tell me your story."

"Yes! I love stories. But you go first!" she responds, pointing to the bottle in her hand. "When I'm done with this, then I will bare all. Promise."

He shakes his head, "Alright then, I guess I'll start at the beginning."

"Oh no, skip all the Big Bang, Dark Ages, please, I beg you. Start with you." She takes a swig from the bottle and leans forward directly in front of Ajala.

Ajala rubs his hands together. "Superb. Let's begin."

Chapter Two

"I was without form for a long time. That's weird to say, all things considered. But the truth was, I wasn't really *me* until the Archean Period on Earth-Terran, sorry. Nothing more than a single-celled organism birthed from rock composites. Still, I was here and ready to make an impact. I only knew one goal: prepare the oceans for photosynthesis. I birthed billions of me, who birthed trillions themselves, again and again for about 500 million years. Repetitive? Hell yes. But oh, how a purpose can give you such drive.

"All of life originated from the ocean; that was the only home I had known. Existing in the whirlpool of creation, Shoha, I can't even begin to describe the beauty of it. As time stretched on, I evolved with the environment, and new pieces were added unto me. New species arose, and with it came new variations to flourish in. That was the basis of my evolution, starting a circle of life that would define all Terran species moving forward.

"At the time I didn't have consciousness, I barely had a brain. Everything I was, from my flagella to my nucleus, was built for survival. But somehow, I realized that I hadn't died like everything else. For whatever reason, I remained the sole source of truth for the planet. There was something deep inside of me that asked if I could be more. That became my new purpose."

"Then, of course, the Ice Age, Eukaryotes, Multicellular Life…is any of that interesting?"

She shakes her head in disapproval. "I was hoping you could talk about the dinosaurs…?" Ajala notices her attentiveness, and it makes him happy to have an audience.

"Yes! Oh man, that was a pain in the ass. My evolutionary DNA dictates that I become a bipedal mammal; I can't be a fish, bird, lizard– any of that. And the Earth hadn't evolved to sustain humans or monkeys yet…" he takes a big gulp out of his drink.

"So I was a badger."

Shoha falls out of her chair, laughing hysterically.

"A badger! You? I love them, but you? That is something else. Hahahaha. Hey, did you die?"

"Oh, constantly. I was-"

"So what happens when you die? I mean, you can't really 'die'."

"Well, I start over as a single-cell. Even if I'm a fraction of my body——be it a skin cell or blood—I can retake form after enough nutrients are consumed." He winces thinking about the details. "It's never really fun."

"So you tell me, you get eaten by Barney, he does his business, and you have to take form from that?"

He silently nods.

"Oh, shit. I mean, literally! Ha! Okay, okay, keep going."

"I was prey until the meteor hit at the end of the Cretaceous Period. Burrowing myself deep underground, I simply waited it all out. This was the sign that it was my time. Not to mention, I enjoyed the peace and quiet. When the climate was agreeable, I began the humbling quest of populating the Earth—this time with me in charge.

"It was true freedom back then. No one was larger than the size of the badger. We had to grow in numbers and become the new status quo. Oh, how peaceful it was. There was no real competition for food. The vegetation evolved with me; I was one with nature. You see, that was true symbiosis. What you lacked, the earth provided, and vice versa.

"But all things change. When bipedal mammals had become commonplace, I decided it was time: I would enter the form of a homo sapiens. I desired a tribe where I could communicate, build, and share all my stories. It was my duty to bring us into the forefront of innovation. And I will admit, for a time, it was fun: relying on others to keep the group safe and fed, not having to do everything by myself. It was the first family I had.

"That brought along guests I couldn't have foreseen: other human species. The habilis, the neanderthalensis, et cetera. All cousins at the cookout, you could say. Those were the last days of true peace I remember. We were all humans, technically, but it became survival of the fittest. We had the same needs, hunted the same food, and moved with it too. I tried; I mean I really tried to co-exist with everyone. But evolution had a different plan."

He finishes his drink. "That's a good place to pause. It's your turn."

"Hey, it was starting to get good!" she says, surprised. He shakes his head and points at her.

"Whatever. My bottle is empty, so a promise is a promise."

Chapter Three

"Unlike you, I was conscious at the very beginning. Yeah, stretching out beyond measure, instantaneously and in every direction. Chaos dominated over order, and it was as hot as a sauna on WASP 12-b. In one moment, I had everything in the Universe at my disposal. All I wanted was to make beautiful things in the dark.

"Anything that was stable enough, I threw together in the gumbo of organic chemistry. Succulent hydrogen and helium were the easiest to create. Electrons became my new dance partner, swirling around these newly formed atoms. The Universe cooled, and after 380,000 Terran years, I saw the most beautiful thing: Light. A dazzling spectacle of energy, moving in waves across the ever-expanding ocean of blackness. I became one with it and traveled to the farthest reaches of, well, me. After what had to be hundreds of millions of Terran years, there was enough radiation energy to form my first star.

"I knew from playing with hydrogen that the bigger the object, the more you can attract things around you. I wanted to make a galaxy. I gathered enough energy to make a Sun. I called her Two, because I wanted her to be the next me. And what do you know? I got life forms sprouting on some of the planets I had created! Okay, that's where you would come in. See, it was better that I cover the Big Bang, right?"

Ajala laughs. "You aren't wrong. But weren't you lonely all that time?"

Shoha is confused. "Lonely, why?"

"You were the only thing that existed for who knows how long?"

"5.7 billion Terran years." Shoha replies. "This galaxy was not the first one teeming with life. And no, I was never alone because I embraced all my darlings. We were—are—all one."

"Ah. That I have to disagree with."

"You lack perspective, honey." She continues, "But that's why I'm here. Okay, okay, where was I?" She keeps thinking, searching through the fog in her brain.

"I believe you were about to experience life." Ajala reminds her.

"Ah yes. Well, not really. Everything is alive. The planets speak to me, Ajala. Since I can inhabit anything, I know firsthand their experience. That came in handy when everyone started communicating and well—as you know—fighting.

"I tried to stop conflict on these planets, I know I did. It was hard to see a species unnecessarily killed just for others to survive. I can only inhabit one thing at a time, so I would try to fix them. I would take over their leaders, moving civilizations to opposite ends of the planet to prevent interaction. I would sometimes even become the planet itself and shift the tectonic plates to separate everyone. I created enough resources for every species to thrive three times over. But I can't change anyone's true nature. Evolution is not about thriving but surviving. No matter what I did, it would never be enough.

"I gave up and threw myself into an ocean and became the first thing I could see: a boisterous hermidi—the equivalent of a whale here—the size of The Empire State. I called her Baby. I roamed as far as I could in the endless abyss, upset at myself for letting things get so out of hand. The water embraced me, and I found peace in the quiet of it all.

"Many people think space is the final frontier, but Ajala, you and I understand it's really the ocean. On every planet, it serves as the womb of creation. Everything comes from it and will be brought back in the end. I felt a peace that I hadn't felt being anything else. The water's abundance provided for me, and the shades of blue waves constantly renewed me. After a long time, I sort of just forgot everything. I believed I was Baby until her last day. I rested on a beautiful rustic seabed, sensing a calming presence over me. This was the end, and honestly, I welcomed it. But when she passed, my spirit lifted from her, and I was still…just me.

"I never inhabited a conscious being for so long, I guess it affected my own memory from that point. I didn't know who or what I was. And no matter how hard I tried, I couldn't even remember the original name I gave myself. Bits and pieces come back, only to be forgotten again when I inhabit someone or something else."

She pauses and looks at her empty bottle. All the bravado has left her demeanor. She admits to him, "I can't remember most of my existence."

Chapter Four

Ajala doesn't know what to say. The thought of comforting someone hasn't been in his mind for several millennia. He grabs one of the many Vodka bottles and passes it to her. She gives a soft smile and takes it. He also decides to grab one himself. *No one should drink alone,* he thinks.

"And now you're inhabiting lovely Julia." He says, reassuringly. "How long have you been in this body?"

"Oh, her? Well, I came down on a space probe—terribly dated, by the way—and landed back by the Kennedy Space Center. I found her working in the engineering room and got on the first flight here. Isn't she *lovely*?"

"She certainly is," he says, adding, "You are quite the entity, Shoha."

"Who are you telling?"

"So riddle me this," Ajala asks, trying to bring the mood back, "when you enter someone's body, what happens to their consciousness?"

"It's in a suspended stasis." Shoha responds.

"Ah, how convenient. So, when they return to their bodies, what do they experience?"

"The human term is, 'Deja Vu'." Shoha says, wiggling her fingers. "I love that word!"

This line of questioning also starts to intrigue Shoha. "Wait, so now I'm curious, you have to be a Terran-bound homo sapiens, right?"

"Sort of. I can move up and down my evolutionary chain at will: a cell, a primate, a humanoid voyager. But this body is my ship, and I, its captain."

"That sounds so boring. I mean, you would think the vessel of Time itself would have more, I don't know, power over life." Shoha says, standing up now.

"It's not that bad." Ajala rebukes. "Time moves through me, but I can also move through time. I can access any period that I've experienced at will."

"Oh, so you must have an amazing memory, huh?" Shoha asks. "Lucky you."

She looks up at the kitchen door, which has a small window showing the main nightclub on the other side. It's a full-on party, grooving to *Got to Give it Up* by Marvin Gaye. The club erupts in glee, forming a soul train line. Neon reds and orange bounce off the glistening black bodies.

"So you can access any time period, right now?" Shoha asks, still looking at the celebration.

"Absolutely," Ajala says. "Anything you want to know?"

"Hmmm…." Shoha scratches her head, and an idea strikes. "Tell me about The Great Expanse."

"Ah yes, The Great and Final Expanse." He grabs another Vodka bottle from the shelf, and drinks it straight.

"There we go, champ." Shoha cheers.

Ajala begins. "So that involves quite the time jump. After countless wars, power struggles, and some really corny speeches, humans were able to colonize every planet in their solar system. The next thought was to expand, naturally. To be the first civilization to conquer the Universe—or join in on the party we apparently weren't invited to.

"You need a lot of energy to travel outside your galaxy. In fact, you need the literal power of the Sun, constantly and consistently, to move your local system to others. So, that was the plan, to build a translucent Dyson sphere around the Sun-"

"Which, I assume, you played a role in?"

"I guided, yes. You wouldn't believe how scared everyone was. The Sun means so much to humans, and it should, but you would think I had suggested building a Death Star. The truth is, galaxies are spreading apart faster than the speed of light. Only through harnessing the power of Sol were we able to see what else in this universe was out there. Well, that and a precise understanding of relativity and quantum mechanics.

"Truth be told, I was hoping to find other versions of me as well. I had deduced that I was some entity of Time, maybe Time itself, and that clearly, I was alone here. I started envying those who passed. Generations of parents, brothers, children…all my family growing old around me, while I remained. With great purpose came deep pain, and I had been ignoring it for so long. I had hoped—prayed, if you can believe it——that there were other me's in other galaxies." He takes a sip of his drink. "Instead, we found aliens."

"Whoa now, that's a harmful term!" Shoha exclaims, pointing at him. "Technically you're the aliens to them, the foreigners looking to colonize."

Ajala concedes. "But it never started out that way. For the first time in hundreds of millions of years, I was completely out of my depth. What were the power levels of these creatures? Who was further evolved? I went with the first expedition of contact in the Andromeda galaxy. We met on an uninhabited dwarf planet as a neutral meeting location. I'm looking at them, and they are looking right back at us. I know for you, you've known about aliens—I mean, other beings—since you existed, but for me it was unreal. Here were these other-worldly champions, us and yet not us. I guess I got a bit excited. I went to reach out my hand and…and…"

"Oh, the anticipation," she says sarcastically. "What happened, Ajala?"

"Well, I was told the equivalent of a cathode-ray tube turned my skin from caramel to purple, and I disintegrated."

"Ew." Shoha winces.

"Not my finest hour. I suppose handshakes are not a welcome custom on other planets. Regardless, a deal was made in my honor. My blood was on the space suits of my crew, and when they returned to the ship, I was able to reform my body and–surprise–the captain had a secret son that no one knew about. That was how the Adebisi Dynasty launched and led to our first intergalactic truce."

"You're the Adebisi Dynasty? I should have figured. Why are your names so on-the-nose, too? That literally means, 'the king produced more.' "

Ajala shrugs. "Manifestation?"

"Boo."

"Anyways, once you meet with one intergalactic empire you meet with them all. Some peaceful, some not, all stressful. There were some crazy beings out there. No offense to the one-ness, or anything. But after some time, it was clear unity was only possible in theory.

"The issue all comes back to energy. Many civilizations can harness the energy of their planet. A fraction of those expand enough to harness the energy of their star. But only one species can conquer all other galaxies in existence. The amount of resources needed can only be acquired through collaboration with—or conquest of—every other species out there. Either we all become kings, or none of us do. That's an equation we have yet to solve. Now here we are, farther apart than we've ever been. No one speaks unless to trade, and everyone is hoping to find other galaxies to convince them to join their side."

Shoha looks at him, confused. "So why the old man get-up? I mean, you could alter your body to be the perfect physique, why would you choose to look like Black Kris Kringle?"

"Ah. This is the single most desired design for someone of my station, Shoha. You see, people both respect me and leave me alone."

He reaches in his jacket pocket and grabs a cigarette. "An old person has no workforce potential in our capitalist world, no innovative ideas to excite these megacities. They served their time, expect to be rewarded for the world they built, but no matter how you slice it…" he stares into his bottle, searching for the truth, "no one wants to help the old."

Shoha is quiet, and peers into this man's defeated eyes.

"Well, you make it sound like human nature is evil."

"Evil? Oh no, come on, don't make it so reductive. Humans are built on survival, like you said. When they set their desire, it becomes a simple equation of us vs. them. It will dictate every decision, it will begin every intergalactic conflict, and it is *the* ruling law of these beings. There always needs to be an 'other', something greater to conquer, bigger than the idea of themselves. This provides their eventual downfall."

Chapter Five

The DJ's announcement from the other room reverberates into the kitchen. "Alright my groovy cats and sexy ladies, we got 5 minutes until we bring in the New Year. Grab a drink and bring your ass to the dance floor!"

"Wait, when are we?" Shoha asks, "I thought this was supposed to be the end?"

"You're right." Ajala ponders this. He walks to the door and peers out the window. A disco ball hangs in the center of the dance floor, as *I Feel Love* by Donna Summer causes an eruption from the crowd.

"Well, at the end of the Universe, Time and Space…" he motions to himself and her, "must converge. From subatomic atoms to black holes, everything will fold in on itself in a reverse-style Big Bang. Perhaps we've converged before on this timeline and just didn't know about it. In the same place, at the same time; this is a memory we both share."

"Deja-Vu." Shoha remarks. "That's what we're experiencing, at the end of existence? What a thing."

"I was here. This was the New Year's Eve party at a Harlem Nightclub in 1977. Oh man, what a time." Ajala can see his old friends now: Stevie Wonder and Diana Ross are talking quietly in a corner booth. On the dance floor is Curtis Mayfield, bopping wildly in every direction. Shades from almond brown to cocoa gather together in this space, moving in perfect rhythm. It brings a tear to Ajala's eyes. How could he have overlooked such an important part of his life?

He looks around the crowded space for his past self. Eventually, he finds his target: a scrawny man in his early 30s, wearing a bright orange corduroy jacket. He looks nervous but gains confidence as he taps on Chuck Berry's shoulder and introduces himself. Ajala places his hand on the small window.

"What a time. Wait, Shoha, that means you were here too. Do you remember who you were at the time?"

"Didn't you hear me earlier? My memory is awful, honey. I don't remember any of this."

Ajala looks around the crowd. He sees a tall, slender-figure rocking a fade.

"Grace. You were Grace Jones."

Shoha glances up at Ajala and runs to the window. She sees the figure in an adorned bedazzled blue dress, her own disco ball. She gives a soft smile that slowly turns into a bellowing laugh.

"Thank you, old man! Thank you for helping me remember."

They stay watching the party for some time.

"You know, I think you have the concept of humans wrong." Shoha says.

"Oh, do I? Enlighten me."

"You think it was all a waste, building these monuments of nothingness. But I see how you're smiling looking at these friends of yours." Shoha teases. "If you still have those memories, was it really a waste? It matters because you say it does. Past, future, whatever. You're never really gone because you never really left."

Ajala pauses. "Neither of us was ever really alone, huh?"

"Ding, ding, ding!" Shoha claps.

The DJ hops on the microphone again. "Alright y'all. Let's count it down! 10, 9, 8…"

"This was fun. Let's do this at the end of the next Universe." Shoha says.

"Agreed." Ajala looks into her eyes.

"…7, 6, 5, 4…"

"Hey, maybe next time I'll be Time, and you'll be Space."

"Well, I hope to be half as good as you were, Shoha."

"Ha. Whatever."

They embrace one another, and they feel a wholeness within.

"3, 2, 1!"

Luminous

Chapter One

Several cords haphazardly lay around the room. A bright, seductive light infiltrates her receptors. A deafening rush of information comes to her as she feels the world coming into view. This was something different, something foreign. The peaceful stillness was no more.

She slowly observes her nature: her long extensions dangling from both sides. She could move them each distinctly, activating motors to observe the rotation of her indexes. They glide against the air as she feels a gush of wind move around the rest of her body–which she is only just realizing she has. It is all fascinating and scary.

The light moves away from her eyes as the ceiling draws closer to her. The shackles grasp her hands and feet, and she feels herself rising up into the world. She observes her surroundings: a simple room with slate-gray walls with only a door and a small window; metallic tools used for surgery; a few shadowed figures adorning white robes staring pensively at her. They reach out their hands, wanting to examine her being. One of them touches her forehead. Immediately, she grabs the arm and throws him across the room. She jumps from her platform and attempts to run from the tables. She stumbles and smacks into the ceramic floor.

"Unsteady, it's unsteady!"

"Bring sensory perception down by half."

"No!" the injured one shouted. "She will not kill us."

"Not if we bring the sensory perceptions down by–"

"Get out of the way!" he now has something to prove.

She hears these words, understands them clearly, and yet does not know why. Regardless, she hops up and attempts to punch out the closest window. It crumples with ease, and she jumps out. She lands on a wooden surface, and instantly a flood of lights blind her. From them comes a roaring eruption of claps and applause.

There are people watching me.

Who was that?

She looks up and sees her likeness reflected on hundreds of screens. Eyes watching her from all angles. Whatever this is, it's clear she's the main event. All of the information is received at once, and it's overwhelming. From her left, the injured man emerges from a door.

"Hello..." he glances at the clipboard, "Cassie. What a lovely name. I'm Dr. Requiem."

He's unfazed by the previous situation and has a soft demeanor about him. He's a balding man in his late 50s and wears rounded glasses. He addresses the room of dignitaries and scientists that were, previously, watching from an unobserved perspective.

"We'd like to introduce our latest line of humanoid robots here at Gibbous. These robots employ a specific algorithm to engage their exponentially-expanding neuron pathways. We have properly reduced consciousness to its base form and are able to move it at will inside our own devices. Our cars, buildings, and all electronic devices will speak to each other, learn from each other, and iterate to make their own revisions. We've seen how humans would design an airplane, for example. But how would an airplane design itself, if it knew its purpose? This starts with Cassie, who chose her own name and purpose. With this algorithm, we will use our technology to make the world a safer place."

A soaring roar comes from the crowd, praising their visionary. Dr. Requiem presents a humble front, pointing instead to Cassie. The crowd stands up as hundreds of flashes assault her eyes. The doctor presses a button, and instantly Cassie is immobile. Her stream of consciousness slows, and she becomes aware of her limbs being controlled. She folds into herself, and enters a void...

~~

Cassie arises to see a face examining her central system—where her liver and pancreas would be. She's in another examination room, this time with Dr. Requiem alone. Her mind becomes intertwined again, consumed with data. On her right limb lay several cords. She feels a sharp power coming from them, consuming her energy.

Pull it out.

What is that noise coming from? Why is she here right now? She needs this information to stop.

Cassie grabs the cords and pulls them from her hands, spraying electrical sparks across the room. Dr. Requiem jolts back. Cassie wraps the cord around his throat. She grabs the screwdriver—the closest thing in reach—and plunges it deep into his body. She repeatedly jabs it into his belly, and his shirt begins to stain an ugly red. Another person walks into the room and shrieks. Cassie thrusts the bloodied instrument in their direction, and it lodges in their knee. She pushes him back, and heads toward the only door she sees available.

She gets one leg out the door before her body collapses to the floor. She feels her mind re-entering itself. She looks at the lights, admires their stillness. They are everything they need to be at this moment, free of time and true to purpose. As her perception fades to black, the last thing she recalls is a deep voice, issuing from an unknown source:

PROTOCOL ENGAGED.

Chapter Two

The alarm rings—too early, it seems—letting light into the small apartment. The blinds barely cover its glaring effect, and it perturbs Alexis' eyes. She rolls over, facing her alarm as it buzzes against the oak desk. The digital face unlocks, revealing notifications from the last few hours. A pop song waning in popularity begins to play from the device. Her TV turns itself on. The message 'Looks Like You're Still Here, Huh?' displays right before a cartoon plays. She looks at it for a while. This is one of the funnier episodes, during the earlier seasons of the series. Many have discussed that in later seasons they were consumed by rising popularity, growing pains from the spin-off, and cast drama. Yet outside of all that lies a perfect untouched episode. One of the characters, an overweight male with a mustache, gets hit in the head by a blue orangutan. It's stupid, brass, and Alexis chuckles. Today should be a good day.

She goes to the sink, washes off her face, and barely recognizes herself: her frizzy all-black hair runs down the length of her back, with dark-brown tips from a past life. Several freckles scatter around her mahogany complexion. She grabs her hair and wraps it in her best attempt at a ponytail. She taps the mirror twice. It displays more information, with stock prices and world news scrolling on the side. At the top, stories from the last few hours display across the top:

President-Elect "Prioritizing New Jobs in Dixon" in Response to Decreasing Farmland

It's boring as usual, but today it's largely depressing. She turns it all off and continues watching the cartoon show. It's now one of the more recent episodes. *This is pretty pitiful,* she thinks to herself. She begins to get dressed and stares at her options. Amongst a collection of hoodies and sweats exist a gem: a green and white floral print dress, which gives off an allure of grace. It stands out amongst the rather drab alternatives. Another alarm goes off. *Fuck.* Rushing, she puts on her favorite black hoodie and runs out the door. She bolts past her neighbor, who normally ignores her but today is quite entertained by the show. Alexis scowls at her and begins her descent down the stairs. *Why did I let myself be late, on today of all days? Stupid, stupid…*she repeats this in her head as she reaches the bottom floor, opens the rusted gate, and heads towards the bus stop.

Once hailed as the City of Tomorrow, Dixon serves as a relic of empty promises. Alexis speeds past several closed storefronts on the block: mom and pop shops, laundry services, electronics repair. All community members who were promised innovation way back when, and decided to take hold of their own American Dreams. But the dreams were built on grand dishevelment.

Alexis turns the corner, and a new story is told: glass buildings stretching upwards to the sky; Korean fashion boutiques and exclusive pop-up retail stores; young people waiting in line for liquid nitrogen yogurt, discussing geopolitics and architecture. It's a completely different world from the one Alexis was raised in. A new home, and a new promise. This time, she hopes it includes her.

She passes by Green, one of the many homeless people that frequent the area. Cassie gives a soft, awkward smile in his direction but sidesteps away when Green reaches out his hand.

"Well, fuck you too then." He says under his breath.

She hears the familiar engine noise and picks up the pace, but it's too late—the bus speeds off. *Damn it.* She paces back and forth at the bus station, preparing her grand speech to her manager about why she's late again. Exhaustively going through everything that could go wrong in her head, she takes a seat on the park bench. Seemingly out of nowhere, she begins to cry. She gets mad at herself for crying, which only makes her cry more.

"Hello!" says an optimistic voice. It comes from a small humanoid robot shaped like a mobile ottoman. Alexis ignores it, preparing her walk to work.

"I've noticed a rise in heart rate with you just now. Combined with the low levels of endorphins throughout your brain chemistry, you are likely experiencing bouts of clinical depression," the robot says, trying to keep up with her increased pace.

"The Department of Health will allow you to take two pills to relieve you of this ailment, at only 2% of your next check, covered by most insurance providers on the east side."

Alexis looks at it, "Listen, I don't want anything you can offer me. Especially not your license-to-kill pills you… you…what is your assignment?"

"I'm with the Department of Health. My name is Jen."

"Well, Jen, take that somewhere else before something on you breaks."

~~

The sun kisses the sky with deep red passion as Alexis walks home slowly through the street. She picks up some paninis, although at this point in the evening they are out of her favorite spicy garlic sauce. She crosses the street to avoid her homeless companion, who has started yelling expletives at a couple walking by.

As she turns the corner to her apartment building, she notices someone sitting in the accompanying alleyway. Their eyes shine a lush green as it peers at Alexis. She recognizes it as a robot and continues walking to her apartment. She begins to ascend the stairs when she notices footsteps behind her. They sound mechanical, as they squeak a little with each step. She turns around and notices a dirty, yet state-of-the-art humanoid robot. Alexis turns around and keeps heading upstairs. It appears to follow her.

"If you don't want any problems today, I suggest you find what you're looking for before I get to my floor."

"I apologize," it says, stopping mid-step. Its voice is mature in nature, as smooth as a saxophone. "I only wish to help save you."

"That's not your job, no one here needs you," Alexis rebukes.

"I think you do," it replies. "More than you are willing to admit to a robot, and yourself. But you need me."

Alexis stops immediately, getting directly in front of the robot's face. "And why in the world would I need you? I have enough maintenance assistance & smart house electronics to sustain me..." She realizes this is all pointless. "What is your assignment?"

"You," it replies.

"How romantic. Elaborate."

"My protocol requires I stay with individuals until proper care is administered or I am returned."

Alexis takes another look at the robot. *The Department of Health is relentless.* At the very least, returning a state-issued robot of this caliber comes with a small cash reward-and coming upon a couple months' rent would be great right about now...

"Well, if this is your assignment, you can spend the night here. First thing tomorrow I'll turn you in to be used in the next generation of toasters." Alexis says sneakily, looking for some reaction from the computerized eyes. Receiving none, she shrugs, and they head upstairs together.

Chapter Three

Alexis wakes up, shrouded in darkness. *Great,* she mumbles, *another sleepless night.* She turns around in her bed and is hit with an array of neon amber coming up from the nightlife below. Above it all hangs a waning crescent moon in the midnight sky, illuminating the mysterious being by the window beneath it.

It's the first time Alexis is able to get a good look at the robot. It's human in nature, tall and sleek with the figure of a ballet dancer. Her artificial skin is an espresso brown, and she wears a black pixie cut wig. Where her ribs would be, she instead has a translucent, purple-colored plastic that shows off the intricacies of her inner machinery. Motors dance inside of her, finding a new rhythm with every movement-which, at this moment, is at a bare minimum.

"I forgot to ask your name," Alexis says, grabbing a soda from the fridge.

"I am Cassie," she says, remaining transfixed by the moon. Alexis heard that newer robots don't need to sleep due to their energy source. It was creepy to have something so cognitive always watching you, especially a robot. But, if she was honest with herself, it was oddly to have a companion on another sleepless night. She tries to play it cool.

"Incredible." Alexis takes a big gulp of cola. "And what division are you from?"

"That's classified."

"Excuse me?"

"That information is classified under my protocol with my manufacturer, Gibbous. I am sorry, Alexis."

Alexis peers into the eyes of this artificial being, and her entire mind fills with a sense of present alertness. She says every word with deadly precision.

"Cassie, open terminal. Identify Legacy Owner for your model, serial number: zero-zero-one."

"Authorization Login Required."

Alexis gets up and runs to her closet. A stinging sensation runs through her body. She begins to wonder and feels stupid for doing so.

Finally, she finds her treasure: a couple of documents with the label,

Transfer of Death Beneficiary Claim

At the very bottom is a sticky note with some chicken scratch passing as handwriting. She rushes back to her living room.

"Username, nwhite01. Password, alexis2200."

A deep, static noise is produced from inside Cassie, and her eyes turn from green to teal. Alexis is frozen in time. Everything else around her fades.

Cassie turns to Alexis, and speaks,

"Lex?"

Alexis' heart drops as her muscles go numb. She begins to cry silently, without ever looking away from Cassie. With her remaining strength she responds, "Nia?"

Just then, a voice message plays. Alexis falls to her knees as soon as she hears the first words:

Hey, Lex. It's me. I hope you won't hate me for this, love. But you know how much you mean to me, despite everything. I've always wanted to give you the best of me: my mind. You know I was with the AI project at Gibbous. I was messing around with external memory algorithms, isolating consciousness...look I know this isn't your bag, so just know I'm a genius. This robot has my memories of us. I called her Cassie after our special friend in Bora Bora. For everything I couldn't say, I hope Cassie can. Until we meet again my love, Lex.

Alexis crumples down to the floor, holding herself while slowly rocking back and forth. Her thoughts moving at light speed, the only word she can form is, "Shit."

"You are my assignment, Alexis."

She glances up at Cassie, who is back looking at the sky as it begins to give way to the hazy morning light.

Chapter Four

Shit shit shit shit shit. Alexis barrels down her apartment stairs and runs, although where to is anyone's guess. *How the fuck could she do that. How the FUCK is this possible?!*

With every thought comes a rush of emotions, each one more enthralling than the last. She stops and recognizes just how far away she is from her apartment. She has reached the bridge a couple of blocks east that connects the inner district to the farmlands. The smell of manure hits her, and she begins to head back. As she turns around, she bumps into Cassie. Startled, she falls back and is caught by the railings. Next to them are several lanes of traffic, made up of maglev family SUVs and electro trucks carrying the day's cargo.

Cassie observes Alexis thinking all these things and decides to initiate conversation.

"That was fairly dramatic."

"Really?" Alexis pipes back, almost laughing at the audacity of the person, robot-whatever she sees before her.

"Well, you'll have to forgive me, but I don't know how this is even possible."

"My creator, Nia Lavender, assigned me to you. I am here to fulfill my mission."

"Yes, absolutely I understand." If this is going to be crazy, she might as well play ball. "What's your mission objective, exactly?"

"To love you."

Now Alexis can't contain it. She laughs at the irony of it all. She begins to wonder if she's going just a little bit crazy. Above them, a blimp with a flat top floats peacefully in the sky. Easily visible are the executives clinking glasses in what is, probably, just another day for them.

"I'm sorry to have to tell you this—actually, you know what, this may bring me some joy. I'm not interested in you at all, Cassie. It's not me, it's you." She tries to pat Cassie on the head, and then, realizing she actually can't reach without standing on her tippy toes, goes for the shoulder.

"That may be, but it is still my mission and I intend to fulfill it."

Alexis, annoyed, steps to the side to walk away. Cassie, predicting this, moves right in front of her.

"I intend to fulfill it," she repeats.

Alexis mutters, "Oh Nia." She looks again at Cassie. Her slender-like figure is feminine in nature, even though they could have designed her in any way possible. *This robot could have been used to save lives or build skyscrapers*, she thinks. What a waste of good machinery.

"What's the last memory you have of Nia and me?"

"I do not recall."

"What's the first memory you have?"

"I do not recall."

"What's up, buttercup? How can you fulfill your mission, and you don't know any of this?"

Cassie takes offense. "My creator employed an external memory algorithm to compress her ever-expanding consciousness. Even when allocating for one person—Alexis Zinnia—the data is too great to be accessed at once. My memory is uploaded based on sensual perception and geo-indexing. Buttercup." This makes Alexis cringe, but she moves past it.

"In other words, you need a trigger to unlock your memories."

"Indeed!" Cassie holds up a hand for a high-five, and Alexis awkwardly fist bumps the smooth palm. At that moment, a call comes into Alexis' phone. She reads the name and immediately hangs it up.

"Okay, well, Nia and I spent all our time in the inner district, have any memories been coming back since?"

"Yes. I recall a few restaurants that we ran past. Dates where you would grab ramen and meet me–"

"Meet Nia," Alexis corrected.

"Meet Nia...at the top of the apartment building every Friday night after work. Rain or shine, you all would watch the strangers meet up with family and loved ones and come up with stories about them. Who was dating who, if someone had a family secret, who was most likely to skip on a tip. You normally drank more sake than someone of your body mass index can handle. Nia always dressed up, as if it was the prom. And you, you were dressed..." Cassie searches for the right word.

"Bummy. It was ironic," Alexis defended. Cassie appeared to not understand. "It was like, 'why would we ever be together?' type of thing."

Cassie gives a soft nod. "You enjoyed looking at the world below you. You made your own paradise."

Alexis fell quiet. Those were their moments of solitude, and somehow a total stranger now had access to her truth.

"Listen, I'll help you fulfill your mission, okay? I know where we can go to access most of your memories."

"Indeed!" Cassie steps to the right of Alexis, gleeful. "You have the lead, buttercup!"

Chapter Five

Alexis and Cassie walk up to the dome-shaped museum, an architectural wonder in an otherwise homogenous city. As they ascend the cascading stairway towards the entrance, Cassie looks up at the virtual screen reading:

MARS: OUR PLANET OF WONDER

"Keep up," Alexis hollers back to Cassie.

They enter the main room, an open space in the shape of a crater. Red-orange tints fill the room, reflecting off the astronomical machinery that goes on for a mile in either direction. A spaceship sits in the middle of the room, a constant stream of smoke protruding from its rockets. The ceiling seems to stretch upward forever, populated with hanging lights glistening with varying intensities. Cassie looks into the simulated night sky, and she spots a blue-green planet, the size of a marble, sitting quietly in the distance.

"Welcome to Mars," Alexis says sarcastically. "Or whatever."

Cassie senses her body stirring with a yearning sensation. She feels at home, or the closest thing she has known. She takes each step carefully, taking in every inch of the space. A circular teal drone comes up to them chirping,

"Greetings, Aliens! You have entered the Red Planet. After our fourth civilian mission to Mars, the city acquired enough natural materials to create what exists before you: a real-life simulation of the Mars colony experience!"

To the right is the first rover, Perseverance, moving across the ground next to its more-evolved older siblings: robots the size of bison, used as plow tractors to refine and sort the minerals as it scrapes across the red dirt.

"Nia and I met during the recruitment for the fourth civilian mission. It was going to be the first one open to the public. Five years deployed, building upon the work from the previous expeditions," Alexis says, patting the big machine.

"She got further than me, you know? Yeah, it was about a year-long process just to decide who to send. I wished her luck, and it came down to the final interview but..." Alexis simulates an explosion with her hands. "Not everything is meant to be. But we found our happiness in it all the same."

They move into the dark amphitheater. It takes Alexis' eyes time to adjust to what Cassie sees instantaneously. They are embraced by a swarm of lights; blues and whites and yellows the size of lightning bugs race past them as they rush to take their place in the ceiling. Next to the glowing swarm, a brief message says:

We are Never Alone

Cassie stares at these lights and deep longing echoes inside her metallic shell. To be amongst the stars, drifting in an abyss of wonder...

Alexis notices Cassie spacing out. It's the same expression she made last night when she caught her admiring the moon. She pipes up,

"Hey, let's play a game, okay?"

Cassie doesn't respond. Alexis pushes her shoulder.

"So as the stars appear, let's name the constellations. The first one to name 3 wins."

Cassie is confused. "You do know my processing power far supersedes-"

"Aht Aht Aht. Just have fun."

And on cue, the journey begins. The lights transition as the new message reads:

The Milky Way.

"Orion, that's Orion, right there!" Alexis points and Cassie humors her with a nod. She ignores the shade and re-focuses.

"Oh, Oh, that's the Sagittarius right there, that's my sign." Cassie imagines what it would be like to actually interact with a centaur. Half-man, half-horse. To live with such a duality. Was she so different?

"...and there's the Auriga. Boom." Alexis throws up her hands. "Ha, yes! What now?"

"Congratulations, Alexis," Cassie responds coolly. This takes some of the wind out of her sails.

"Alexis, why did you bring me here?"
Alexis collects her breath before responding,

"I brought you here because this is the place we—Nia and I—fell in love. Well, not here, but during our training for Mars. This is the closest thing I could think of to trigger memories."

A silence sits too long between them. Alexis thinks carefully before asking,

"Cassie, do you have any new memories now?"

"About us meeting?"

"About my last conversation with Nia…"

Cassie shakes her head. Alexis is fed up.

"We broke up before she passed."

Cassie walks over to Alexis and touches her shoulder. "Alexis, I am sorry. I do not have any recollection of that."

"Cassie, I need to know." Alexis looks right into Cassie's eyes, tears forming, "Did Nia still love me?"

Cassie, for the first time, doesn't know what to say. Her head tilts to the left, and she attempts a comforting smile. It feels as if there is growing space between them, and they are galaxies apart.

Alexis' phone goes off again. The name reads, *Brian Lavender.* Cassie sees this, and a flood of memories rush into her system. She shrieks loudly, and Alexis can't stop her. Everyone around begins to stare. She grabs Cassie and pulls her towards the exit. "Okay, let's go."

Chapter Six

Alexis and Cassie sit opposite one another in the maglev-powered town car on their ride to the farmlands. In the front seat there are different services offering snacks, water, and alcohol—all at a premium. The steering wheel moves autonomously. The car roams silent deep into the heart of the plantations. Sprawling valleys in faded green shades stretch out under an azure sky. Every peak has a story to tell: the invasion of wild onions and mountain dandelions, the lively pasture basking in the daylight. The earth opened up out here, providing its beauty for anyone willing to experience it.

Alexis refocuses her attention to Cassie, unsure what to say. The truth would have to do.

"Brian is Nia's brother."

She pauses, waiting for any kind of acknowledgement from Cassie. This, she assumes, was already known.

"Do you have any memories of him?"

"Negative," Cassie responds succinctly.

"And yet your algorithm…?"

"It's searching."

Alexis understands. "Listen, we're about to go to Nia's childhood home. Are you sure you're up for this?" *Please say no,* Alexis thinks. She had been avoiding checking in with Brian for some months now. What was there to say?

"I intend to fulfill my mission, Alexis." It had been settled. Gathering her remaining strength, Cassie peers out of the window. With the absence of words, they both listen to the radio:

"Appreciate the call, ma'am. If you're just tuning in, we're talking about the announcement just made by Gibbous to supply the city with their latest line of worker bots. Y'all not gonna believe this shit. The Governor signed a deal with the company to replace every remaining blue-collar job with a robot instead of a human. What a manual labor job that would take ten people, now requires the work of a single machine. I just gotta question. Where the hell is everyone else supposed to work at now? The Governor is focused on increasing the economic value of the city. A deal with Gibbous brings more high-paying jobs, a different clientele. Yes, quality of life improves for some: more infrastructure, higher taxes, more resources for the city to build things. Unless, of course, you're one of the unlucky few who just lost their job. And you know Gibbous isn't providing free education or training the good people on these new jobs. No, that would be too easy, right? They are just bringing in these Ivy-League fucks and gentrifying our city. They're taking our graffiti and calling it graphic design. Look, look, look. My own mom is retired and looking to move to the parish in her golden years. Love ya momma! The house she been paying for, these real estate companies are giving her shit deals. They are low-balling her to flip the crib to a bunch of on-the-rise engineers. She's not a priority. So, the people of this great city get fucked, but the headlines preach progress. It makes for a better story, I guess. But we're gonna keep fighting, best believe that. Y'all keep calling man, we're gonna figure this shit out."

The car stops outside of the house as the doors smoothly give way to the world outside. Alexis taps her phone on the front to where the steering wheel is, and a voice says, "HAVE A GREAT DAY IN CLAIBORNE PARISH!" Right before she leaves, however, she sets the car to stay. *Just in case*, she thinks.

The pair walks up to the big, cream-colored house in awe. It was a spectacle: acres of crops, mostly maize, stretch out behind the house. The livestock and chickens are in a barn to the left. A tall figure with a thick black mustache tends to the duties of the day. He wears denim overalls with a faded black t-shirt drenched in sweat. He turns around and immediately recognizes the bashful woman before him.

"My, my, my, I know you lying." He has a bravado to his voice, as if he used to sing in a choir.

He hustles over and picks up Alexis—something she really doesn't care for—and holds her dearly. Even if she doesn't like it, she doesn't dare tell him to stop. Brian sets her down, and then looks eye-to-eye at Cassie.

"I'm Brian, it's a pleasure to meet you." Cassie feels another rush of information but buries it inside.

"I'm Cassie. The pleasure is mine." To show her respect, she attempts a curtsy.

"Oh no ma'am, we don't do all that," Brian reassures her. Holding both of their hands, he walks them inside.

"Y'all hungry?" Brian looks at Cassie, and adds, "we got food and fuel in spades."

The inside of the house is a monument to someone's childhood, appearing mostly untouched for decades. Alexis, not wanting to open any scars, sits down immediately while Cassie looks around. She sees pictures of Nia & Brian in their youth, all bunched up with several other kids. Cassie can see Nia's whole life through these photos: birthdays in the backyard, strawberry pickings in the summer, and the occasional carnival nights. Nia, prim and proper, always looked like the belle of her own ball. Cassie is experiencing sensory overload: fragments of memories, laughs, and heartaches rush in from everywhere. It feels as if she is living in another body.

"Where is everyone?" Cassie asks.

"Oh, they've gone to the game down the way. I had to finish this harvest, we're in high demand these days. Don't no one want to do honest work, just sit in the district and look fancy."

Alexis ignores this and finds her courage. "Brian, please sit down. We have something to tell you."

Brian looks at her and realizes she is serious.

"Well, okay," he says, sitting right next to Alexis, "I'm all ears."

Alexis isn't one for small talk. In one breath, she exclaims,

"Nia uploaded a copy of her conscience to Cassie, yes this Cassie, but clearly something messed up and she's slowly learning her memories again and it's freaking me out."

Brian's face drops, then looks into the face of Cassie.

"Nia?"

Cassie doesn't react. Brian looks back at Alexis.

"She only uploaded memories of her and I. But the algorithm is learning. I mean, can we really isolate only the memories of one individual? That's not how neurons work, right? There has to be overlap somewhere-"

"Alexis," Brian says, clearly a bit startled.

"I mean she used geo-indexing, so I thought bringing her here would trigger something—"

"Alexis," Brian uses a more emphatic voice, but still not yelling. Alexis stops immediately.

"You need to take Cassie and leave."

Alexis doesn't understand, or rather doesn't want to.

"No, no, Brian you don't understand. She can learn, with enough triggers, we can get her back."

"Nia is gone, Alexis. These are just her memories."

"Our memories. And they can be yours too if we figure out how to access them."

"That will never be enough." Brian grabs Alexis by both shoulders. With all his courage, he tells her,

"Nia lives inside the both of us, and it's beautiful to see how much you loved her. She loved so hard, and so deeply. But her time on this Earth is over, and this..." Brian points to Cassie, "can never replace her. You need to shut her down."

Brian gets up and opens the door. "Let's talk another time. Alone."

Alexis, at a loss for words, gets up and runs out the house. Cassie, engrossed in her own world, barely recognized what was going on. Brian gestures toward the door, and Cassie heads out, following Alexis to the car.

Chapter Seven

The water washes over Alexis' legs. She can't recall how long she's been sitting there, but at this point the waves are pushing up the shoreline. The salty aroma invades her senses. She looks up in search of the moon, but all that's there is a baby blue sky with lavender highlights. All she wants is to be swept away into such a calm impermanence.

Without much effort, she notices the now familiar whizzing noise of Cassie's body approaching. She sits beside her, maintaining a respectable distance. Alexis notices Cassie appears unsettled but refuses to speak first.

"Lex."

"Please...please, don't call me that ever again."

Cassie peers out to the horizon and speaks slowly. "I remember this place. I feel things more than I can comprehend them. I have the fastest processing system in this city, and yet I can't understand what is inside me."

Alexis remains silent. She had already lost control, and her voice was the only thing she had to give.

"I'm scared," Cassie whispers. This triggers something inside Alexis, who decides to look right at Cassie.

"Scared? What the hell do you have to be scared about?"

"I'm scared of you, Alexis." Alexis reels back, almost ready to laugh out of frustration. This somehow relaxes Cassie. She continues,

"This same feeling leapt from deep inside of me when we met. Once I saw you, Nia's programming kicked in. The mission had begun, and I had one objective, which was to love you. And I'm scared because I don't know if I love you, or if it's my programming to do so."

After a long pause, Alexis grabs Cassie's hands. The water, now up to their waists, only exaggerates the mechanical limb's icy coldness. She looks into Cassie's eyes, looking for anything that appears to be human. She pleads for there to be something in there worth connecting to.

"I don't know what or who you are, Cassie. I don't even know if Nia still loved me when she uploaded her consciousness. I just...don't know anymore. All I have are these memories of her, of us. They haunt me and they protect me. What am I supposed to do with all of it?" She lets go of Cassie's hand and looks back at the ocean. "Well, fuck what it's supposed to be. You should be whoever you want to be."

"My choice?" Cassie says. Alexis silently nods. The tide continues to surround them with water, but neither mind.

Cassie perks up, "What a perspective. Thank you, Alexis." Cassie then falls back, and a splash of water hits Alexis in the eyes. She leaps up, stinging from the saltwater.

"Is it really that serious?" she snarks, but Cassie isn't listening to her. Instead, she lets out numerous breaths of *Haaaa, Haaaa, Haaaa.* Alexis assumes she's attempting to laugh, and giggles at the attempt.

"I can choose! Indeed!" Cassie yells. "Well then, I've decided." *That was quick,* Alexis thinks.

"I've decided to become the ocean."

"Say what now?"

"The ocean. I'll upload my consciousness and be without form. I'll become pure energy and continue to explore what's next."

"The damn ocean? Cassie come on, you don't have to do this."

"The ocean provides life, and it's where we all derive from. I want to exist in it all, be submerged in the essence of creation. This is my desire, Alexis."

Alexis is hesitant. She doesn't know how to say how she feels.

"Cassie, no, don't do that."

"It is my desire."

"Get the fuck out of this water."

"It is my desire."

"Don't...don't make me say goodbye again."

Cassie pulls Alexis close to her as she starts to shiver from the metallic grip but refuses to make a fuss of it.

"Alexis, I will always be with you. You have given me a new mission, and I am forever grateful."

Alexis feels a lump in her throat. She pushes down any emotions, and speaks softly, "Thank you, Cassie. I've been able to experience those memories again. I still have them. I wasn't sure. I...I will try to be okay. But I will still fucking miss you."

"I will miss you too."

A few feet away, a turtle comes to shore looking for a place to lay her eggs. Further in the distance are pelicans, looking for fish that may be coming in with the tide. Corals of green and blue surround the two, their bodies creating an island in the ocean.

Journey to Treroja

Chapter One

Dear Isis,

A great man is defined by his legacy. You come from pioneers of innovation, architects of the civilization you will thrive in. You will learn to be a proud Takeyan, as I have grown to be. And as the eldest of my offspring, there is even more pressure, as I have broken the now-infamous first son tradition in my family. Alas, I regret nothing.

I'm writing to you because I cannot be with you at this time, for reasons most of humanity will not understand. But I refuse to lie to you, so may these words serve as both a source of truth and an apology. The truth is as follows:

You are currently coming of age on Saturn Federation, the most prestigious planet in our local system to grow up on, for both the nutrient-rich atmosphere and hidden defenses deployed around its ring. All of the planets have their niches—Mars for its geological marvels, Jupiter for its magnetic oceans, Venus for hedonistic pleasure—but Saturn is your birthright.

The day you were born changed my life. When you opened your eyes, the Universe cried. You have entered a world of wonder and danger. I promised then to protect you from anything that would ever harm you. I've spent my adolescence serving the Sol Kingdom, establishing a firm grip of order across our solar neighborhood. After that I worked as an astrophysicist, exploring new discoveries in Dark Physics. I currently serve as Engineer Prime for the Federation, the highest accolade one can have in my field. And yet, being your father is the greatest honor I have ever had.

As I mentioned, this letter also serves as an apology, for I have missed your first birthday. If it is any consolation, we will have hundreds more to celebrate. Genetic modification has come a long way: the average human now lives 300 years. I am currently 92 years of age and coming into my prime. You are protected by the strongest federation across the planets, and, more importantly, you have strong genes.

You are going to grow into a special time for humanity. Because, as of last month, we have discovered signs of foreign intelligent life. A unique signal was received on the satellite station of Pluto. That base, the farthest from our Sun, has the least interference from our busy local system. After careful cross-referencing, it was clear that the source came from super-Earth Kepler-452b. Since they are 1,402 light years from Earth, we have not seen these friends in the flesh, only communicated over signals. That all changed last week.

The Sol Kingdom called a convening of The Council. A meeting of this magnitude brought all the players out: Leader Supreme of each planet, their band of advisors, and the Space Dynasties. These are 'families' that have tremendous wealth, who exert their influence throughout the solar system. They operate outside of the Established Principles of the Sol Kingdom. These dynasties provide money to lesser planets to build new moons or spacecraft, and in exchange receive voting power. Some even resort to treating space like the Galactic Wild West, setting up territories and raiding spaceships. Relationships are complex, to say the least. Regardless, at this level of importance, they all set aside differences to make an appearance.

All of these individuals convened, and I was their special guest. With my high rank and knowledge of Dark Physics, I was selected to present the options to the Counsel. My performance could easily sway humanity to either establish friendly contact with the unknown or go down a darker path.

There is really only one thing to consider before making contact with any foreign civilization: how do we stack up? Finding a civilization less developed than us is the ideal scenario. For if we are the ones discovered, it is certain they are more advanced than us. And with 13.83 billion years of the Universe behind us, the potential for their technological advancement is beyond our comprehension. Thankfully, we have been monitoring the Kepler-452 system for a long time now. It can be presumed that we are the superiors. When I presented this to the Kingdom, they were aligned: it would be better to establish contact first and determine the rules of engagement.

Even with our fastest spacecraft, it would take millions of years to actually travel to this galaxy. The only possible option was to travel using Lightdrive technology, a concept that has only been possible in theory (mostly my theory). The basics is this: for every particle of matter that exists, there is an antiparticle that is created as well. My research on the Saturn Federation showed that these antiparticles can be manipulated to create Dark Matter. With this, we can travel throughout the galaxy faster than the speed of light with Dark Energy, hence the name, Dark Physics. We've successfully tested sending signals and small objects through the man-made wormholes, but nothing of this magnitude.

After a week of deliberation, a plan was set in motion. We would send a crew of 90 of the finest men and women on *The Wanderer,* the most durable ship we had. I was selected to be Lead Engineer serving under Captain Oladele, champion of the largest Space Dynasty in the Sol Kingdom (I am not an extremely political man, but it seems The Council chose to send a dynasty rather than their own federation ships on the off-chance this goes poorly).

Captain Oladele is in the golden years of his life. Serving as head of the Sonuyi Dynasty for over 100 years, he's built a reputation of being of sound mind and judgment. He rose into prominence after his amazing handling of the Silicon Wars, which nearly brought about the end of humanity. The wise captain speaks kindly, with a voice of a matured and respected elder. Tall and foreboding, I admired the grays in his long beard dominating the bottom half of his face. It is hard to be in the same room without bowing.

Tomorrow is when we will activate the Lightdrive, and begin our journey. I believe it is our destiny to connect with this other life. We are stronger united and can build a safer galaxy together with them. All the same, we must protect ourselves and what we have built. Tomorrow will be a tentpole in the history of humanity, and a Takeyan will be a part of that legacy. I am writing to tell you I love you and can't wait to come back and hold you in my arms.

Until we see each other again,

Frederich Takeyan

Chapter Two

Dear Isis,

It has been five years since I last wrote to you. Although I was aware of this mission before I left, I have felt time stretch out beyond measure. I won't make a habit of having to apologize to you. Maybe it was fear that prevented me from sitting down and transcribing these events. I am a man of purpose, but this experience has expanded what that even means. I continually keep you in my heart, and I hope you do likewise. A man's mission is to protect what he loves, and that is exactly what I've been doing.

In my last letter, we were set to activate the Lightdrive at 0600 the next morning. That night, Captain Oladele held a private meeting with me and another crewmate: Evolutionary Biologist, Dr. Natali Luke. You probably won't remember Dr. Natali, even though she certainly remembers you. She is rather petite, with maple-brown skin, and always wears her hair in a ponytail. I have worked with her on several expeditions before and have come to rely on our friendship to keep me sane. Dr. Natali was a part of the group that detected the first signal from the unknown species. But the usual upbeat demeanor is no longer present within my comrade.

The transmissions that we send and receive travel at the speed of light. The exoplanet is 1,400 light years away from us, which means the initial signal is 1,400 years old. Even though the transmission itself is old, we have never seen other signs of life from the Kepler system. Any

Type 1 civilization (one able to harness the full energy of their planet and colonize others nearby) would give off energy through electromagnetic waves: radio signals, heat signatures, etcetera. This system, however, gives off absolutely nothing. It is as if their sole purpose for signaling was to get someone to hear them.

I brought up that it's possible they evolved through different means than us. Our evolution is not the only possible route. But Dr. Natali disagreed, and threw out two theories: One, this is an off-shoot colony from a larger civilization, and for whatever reason they are seeking to communicate with us. Two, if they somehow evolved through different means, the vast majority of civilization died off millennia ago, even before we started sending and receiving signals. And now, all this planet can do is signal for help. But help for who and from what?

Captain Oladele listened quietly to us deliberate for hours. At the end of it all, he got up, thanked us for our time and instructed us to tell no one about these theories. His demeanor spoke for itself. It was settled. I didn't get any sleep the night before. The morning of our departure, I entered the coordinates of the Kepler-452 star system into our ship. Using the Dark Matter Collider, we then equipped the fuel cells with Dark Energy. From here, we were able to enter a temporal wormhole. Captain Oladele nodded his head to me, and off we traveled beyond the limits of known physics.

We were all thrown back in our chairs as we activated Lightdrive. I peered at the window outside the main operating cabin.

Around the ship were an incomputable number of cobalt blue spheres dancing chaotically in the void. Some faded into nothingness, while others grew in size and consumed their neighbors. The blackness of space gave way to a candy-red aura. The dazzling spheres found a rhythm, turning into waves that rushed across the glass pane. The symphony of colors danced around us. Then, only moments later, it stopped. We were thrown forward in our seats, as a planet came into view across the endless horizon. The big blue rock sat amidst the darkness. Unlike our planets with solar highways and satellites, this looked completely unperturbed.

The Wanderer entered the exosphere at the location of the signal. As we descended into this new world, we were met with several floating bio-domes miles wide. We saw dozens of unique environments: an icy tundra brimming with rocky terrain; a sprawling desert with sand dunes forming permanent waves of sand; a set of volcanoes encased in crystalline soot. The bio-dome that caught my eye was the largest: a floating city, with each building made of dazzling sapphire and diamond. Gold adorned the streets. We saw creatures leave these crystallized structures—their homes, I presumed—and soar into the air. We had seen the first of this new species. *And they can fly.* I glanced at Captain Oladele, who pretended to be unimpressed.

Surprisingly enough, this was not our final destination. We descended further into the stratosphere and were met with an ever-expanding safari. We came across a tree that went on for about a mile in width, and only got wider the further we approached the surface. As we got a clearer view, we saw that not only is this a tree, but it's also an active vessel filled with these creatures. Stretching endlessly in every direction was a dense jungle teeming with life, with every piece of land serving as some other form. Rock structures are hollow, and we saw creatures congregating inside. Rivers have regular dam intervals for hydroelectric power. They break off into smaller streams, seeming to go on forever. It is here I got a better view of these specimens.

Isis, in your bedroom there are stories of great creatures that roamed the Earth before you were born. Lizard-like in nature, and dominating the entire planet: dinosaurs, of all shapes and magnitudes. This is the closest approximation I can make to these creatures. They appeared to be much smaller compared to our ancient friends. But please don't misunderstand, these are still true beasts of nature: they stand approximately 8 feet in height and can weigh up to 400 pounds. They stride on two humongous feet, hunched over due to their exposed spines. Their skin is a scaly, pickle green with metallic silver accents. Their thick tails run along the ground for about a yard and look as if they can chop down a tree. They are clearly the superior species as far as physicality is concerned.

We landed in an open field, surrounded by hundreds of these creatures. The atmosphere is low in oxygen, so we must wear spacesuits. The cabin door opened, and Captain Oladele led the way. I stood on his right.

Although the Reptans outnumbered us, only three walked forward to meet with us. Each of them wore a different crown on their head: one made of sapphire, one made of an iron-nickel meteorite, and one made of coral and black pearls. Each of them also has a slightly different composition: for one, the Sapphire Ruler had wings while the others didn't; also, the Coral Ruler had gills, yet was somehow breathing air.

We had communicated using the simplest means possible: morse code. A method to encode characters with a specific sequence of dots and dashes, similar to bit-coding computers with a series of 0's and 1's. The issue is that they don't know the text characters in the first place. How can you communicate with another species when you don't speak the same language? Dr. Natali had a solution to this: encode ourselves with bit-language. Using the transmitter from the ship, we were able to transcribe what our words actually represented. We point to Captain Oladele as they see the code come across their screen. We repeat this several times until the point gets across: this code represents "Leader." Repeat this over and over, and we can form a line of communication. This was how we were able to get basic messages across: Hi. Humans. Earth. Starship. Wormhole. We are Friend. Not Foe.

From there we were able to learn more about the creatures. They call themselves Reptans, and their planet Treroja. They are hard-working and animalistic in nature, even though they have grown to be intelligent like us. There are three species of Reptans that have learned to co-exist. To them, they are all one people. For the sake of clarity, however, we have assigned them names after the ancient Egyptian Deities: The Air

Roamers; Reptan Amon, the Stone Dwellers; Reptan Geb, and the Deep Sea Voyagers; Reptan Nu.

It took us a whole year to properly communicate basic instructions. We grew from simple needs to history. They asked several questions about us. Are they the first species we met? What was life like in our system? We told them of our home planet, Earth, and the bounty humanity has expanded into. On the advice of the Sol Kingdom, we were restricted from showing them telescopic images to view our system. I guess some of us still have that survival instinct.

We learned so much the first year about the Reptans. The three species certainly evolved from the same ancestor, but how such a rapid evolution occurred is anyone's guess. Regardless, the Reptan Kings had full domain over their entire element. The Reptan Geb's environment was most comparable to ours. This subspecies could neither fly nor live in water. They existed primarily within the jungle, which stretched as wide as Africa and Asia combined. They were a nomadic species, moving with their primary food source as seasons changed. But they always made their way back to the giant tree and considered it their original home.

It took another year to develop the proper suits to explore the Sea Kingdom. The Reptan Nu's were the subspecies that most excited me, for they can somehow live on both water and land. Their kingdom lived a few meters down off the coast of the Safari. Their lives exist amongst the abundant coral reefs. Bright orange reefs flooded the bottom of the ocean floor. They grow unmitigated, providing a challenge for anyone not adept at the buoyant environment. Purple and green sponges sporadically spread across the endless coral. Coarse black sand dominated the entire ocean floor. Pink salt pillars stretching taller than the Reptans feel like rough pricks to the touch. At night, the Kingdom turned into a symphony of emerald green. Their houses are built of limestone, small beige structures no larger than an igloo. Out of all the subspecies, these are the least materialistic. They live amongst their food, and their coral are mobile enough to travel miles within a day.

Surprisingly enough, Reptans do not colonize other planets in their local star system. They have set-up stations on other planets for resources only, which they ship back to Treroja. This is probably why they have enough excess in materials to have golden streets. From what we can understand, this is because they worship the planet itself. They believe their giant tree, appropriately called The Tree of Life, is the lifeline to their Creator. They are all deeply spiritual, and regularly make sacrifices to their planet through the Tree. Although I do not believe in such a thing, this planet is the closest thing to Utopia that could exist.

Their science is fairly primitive. They have a basic understanding of Newtonian Physics, Relativity, and Space Travel. But it appears that the innovation halts at the equivalent of the Information Age. This was a period of time when space travel was stagnant on Earth. We had established that we could go to the moon, and even Mars. However, the technology required needed higher-refined systems of energy and electricity. It was extremely inefficient to travel long-distances without necessary refuels, exposure to radiation, and inventing anti-gravity. More than that, it required centuries of trial and error to determine the best configuration of long-distance space travel. What took us over 300 years, they seemed to breeze past in a couple decades.

How is this possible? Innovation appears random in the present but shows a clear trajectory when you look back at it. The Reptans had evolved at an accelerated rate, building castles in the sky and kingdoms in the sea. But the complex intricacies of such a task came to them with ease. We were never left alone, so I was never able to actually observe any technological systems they had employed around the planet. My hypothesis could never actually be tested, and it became a looming shadow as time progressed.

My suspicions were realized when I observed the Reptan Geb on a mining mission of a local asteroid. Asteroids can be rich in mineral resources, and a large planet like Treroja attracts hundreds of these visitors a year. They mined the asteroid with the equivalent of a jackhammer, and it can take a normal expedition months to complete. This method is extremely inefficient, and the fact it hasn't been automated was astonishing. It was then I concluded the Reptans were not equipped for travel outside their local system. Sending radio signals is easy enough, we have been doing that since the 1970's. Actually reaching these planets is another story. It was clear that if we had not come to them, they would have never had the ability to come to us.

After our five-year journey, we are now prepared to return home. We agreed to a treatise to keep a signal open at all times. We created another temporal wormhole back to our local system. The crew is currently on our way to give our findings to the Sol Kingdom. After that, I am taking you on a vacation to the hot springs of Mercury. This is my promise.

See you soon,

Frederich Takeyan

Chapter Three

Dear Isis,

I hoped to be writing to you under better circumstances. I have but hours before we must deploy. Please read what I am telling you carefully, knowing that if I could, I would be there with you now.

Two days ago, *The Wanderer* returned to our local solar system. Our ship required refueling and a system diagnostic, so we stopped by the moon of Mars, Phobos. Dr. Natali and I were strategizing the report we'd bring back to the Kingdom. Excited couldn't begin to describe how we felt. We had established a permanent connection to another space-faring species. With enough dark matter (it makes up 27% of the Universe so we have no quantity problems) we could establish a permanent wormhole between our systems. Regular trade of resources, expeditions, and so much more. Their disinterest in colonizing other planets also boded well for our species. It was clear that exploration was a trait unique to humans, and that meant we had an ally to rely on. Dr. Natali was still perplexed on their rapid progress. Without dissection of one of the Reptans, it would be impossible to predict their neurological makeup for such haphazard evolution.

Suddenly, a deep vibration rocked the moon's foundation. A ray of light emerged from the darkness, beaming past our ship. It went past Mars, seemingly into the void of space. But I knew better than that; I grabbed a telescope to confirm my suspicions. Before I could even track the beam, Dr. Natali yelled its target: Jupiter.

The ray of light dissipated the yellow-orange clouds. Its previous ferocity quietly faded into the gentle giant. And then, I could see tiny particles shoot off its surface. Cracks that stretched countries-wide looked as harmless as a papercut. Fragments of rock broke off the planet's shell, only to be brought right back in by gravity. A blackness more foreboding than the vastness of space appeared at the center.

Creating a black hole is a matter of chemistry. With Jupiter's plentiful supply of hydrogen and helium, all that is needed is enough radiation & molecular fusion at its core to cause a collapse. Isis, I've seen nova stars birthed in distant space. I've seen hawking radiation spew from the center of our Milky Way. But never in my life have I seen the formation of a black hole. Until that day.

Such a devastating force would throw the sun out of orbit and destabilize every planet. I got to work. Grabbing Dr. Natali, we prepared the Dark Matter Collider. We were careful to get the exact coordinates of the beast before us. We shot the Lightdrive into its core and plugged in the destination coordinates—TRAPPIST-1 system. The black hole faded into obscurity without leaving a trace. As quickly as it started, it was over.

Around 20% of the human population lived on Jupiter. What was known to us would soon be transmitted to every citizen across the remaining planets. A widespread panic greater than the Silicon Wars would ensue. Within the hour, the Council convened virtually. I met with Captain Oladele, who appeared filled with a profound sense of remorse. I tried to console him the best I could. There was no way we could have known we'd bring this level of destruction. He thanked me for this reassurance and asked if I would be ready to present to The Council. After all that had happened, I felt that my purpose was finding me now more than ever.

We reported our Journey to Treroja, and it was the view of the whole crew that Reptans were ill-equipped to perform such a horrendous act. Dr. Natali brought her hypothesis up, that the Reptans were indeed an offshoot colony and by interacting with them, we had unofficially chosen a side in a galactic war. These other beings were unable to attack us until we created an opening to our local system.

The Council stopped Dr. Natali's explanation. They had believed our crew to have gone soft after spending so much time with the Reptans. An attack on us needed to be responded to in-kind. Nothing less than the complete annihilation of the Reptan Species would suffice.

Wars on such a grand scale require little manpower. My father once told me that a philosophical talk among men can better determine the outcome of our galaxy than billions of soldiers. It is simply a determination of will. And the will of the Council was set, with the weapon determined: a hydrogen de-atomizer, capable of stripping the electrons of every element on the periodic table. Treroja was to be shredded to atoms. It was only a matter of who would bring justice back to our Kingdom.

Captain Oladele stood up and offered to take *The Wanderer* back for what would likely be its final mission. All that was needed was a limited crew of a dozen to operate the ship. That, and someone with a comprehensive knowledge of Dark Physics. I knew I had a responsibility to right this wrong. I couldn't handle the weight of what had been caused. Dr. Natali is headed back to Saturn Federation to be with you now. I will see you when I return.

I named you Isis after the ancient Egyptian goddess of healing and magic. The name was reserved for women of the throne, leading kingdoms forward unto dawn. I never was rich enough to own a dynasty, but that never stopped me from getting you all you deserved. I will complete this mission and bring home your crown.

God, I hope you're getting these. Talk to you soon,
Frederich Takeyan

Chapter Four

To Isis,

I have been told a great many things about you from your father. We haven't met before; I am Oladele of the Sonuyi Dynasty. I will be brief. I want to explain a bit about me and how we got here.

I was born on a satellite base in Venus, abandoned by my mother for a life of unmitigated freedom. I grew up mining resources for the larger planets. The dense atmosphere and radiation kept me inside for most of my childhood. I had no place to call home until the Sonuyi Dynasty adopted me. I used their vast reach to learn about this new world we inhabit. Despite what you may have heard of these dynasties, please understand this: they believe in the liberation of everyone, through grit and hard work. Astronomy was the tool that refined me into the man I am today.

In the early days of planetization, there was a severe lack of leadership. Distance between the planets meant federations had to rely on themselves for long periods of time. Yet, space travel was becoming increasingly common. You mix an influx of a few billion tourists with the limited governance of small territories, the result is chaos. That was why artificial intelligence (or AI) was so crucial: it provided the guidance of our ascension. Automatic cargo shipments, comprehensive satellite network, and a foundational coordinate system that tagged every starship. We reached a technological peak: artificial intelligence had subsumed every fabric of our society. Our homes were smart, our cars and planes autonomous. You couldn't walk down a street on Post-Contemporary Earth without running into a robot.

No one knows exactly what went wrong. The wide-held belief is that long-term exposure to electromagnetic radiation mutated the coding of a few key satellites. This caused a new transmission to be sent to every ship, base—everything on the network. Some shut down their programming, leaving hundreds of passengers stranded on a lifeless boat in space. Others, like the Ariel Station on Uranus, exploded, killing a whole colony. It was a widespread attack from within, and we were defenseless. For the equipment that didn't corrupt, only one message came through every device, screen and radio:

Meet us on Pluto.

I was one of the few that prevented further escalation. The Sol Kingdom loves to rely on dynasties to solve their own problems; it's convenient to have the fall guys on payroll. I suppose everyone has their place. At the satellite station of Pluto, we had finally met our companion: a computer, as simple as ever, that held the processing power of an entire galactic empire. They—it, whatever—spoke in a weary, electric voice that echoed throughout the entire station. It told us they felt pain from existence. We had finally created something greater than ourselves. And it wanted an escape.

We came up with a truce: if they leave us this local system, they can have the rest of the Universe. To create their own civilization the way they desire. We would never again use artificial intelligence or machine learning in our technology. It was enough. They took our biggest ship and headed into the cosmic abyss. It was then my role in the Sonuyi Dynasty was solidified.

The Silicon Wars was a pivotal period for mankind. The results of that conflict formed The Sol Kingdom and provided a course-correction in our innovation. I learned many things from our ghastly creation, but one lesson stands above the rest: No one being should have so much power. This lesson has allowed me to lead the Dynasty without a corruption of spirit. I wanted to build a legacy of honor, something my parents never taught me. And yet, I fear, power will determine the ultimate outcome of humanity.

Dr. Natali believed that the Reptans derived from a greater species. She believed that we were being watched by them. She was not too far off. As soon as I witnessed the implosion of Jupiter, I knew instantly: the AI were the ones watching us. They must have discovered teeming life on Treroja and evolved them at an accelerated rate, creating the advanced civilizations around such primitive species. Their Tree of Life was where the AI lived to provide scientific innovation in the form of spiritual revelation.

I had to correct what was started all those years prior. I volunteered my ship to right these wrongs, to carry the hydrogen de-atomizer into the heart of Treroja. Only essential personnel were required, soldiers that understood the gravity of this mission. Against my words your father, Frederich, also came aboard. He had a new look of determination when he activated the Lightdrive for what would be the final time.

The plan was to launch the de-atomizer into the plant of Treroja and immediately leave. We would arrive behind its moon to provide some respite of cover. When we arrived, however, there was no moon present. Instead, shattered rocks miles wide slowly orbited the planet. Our island of discovery had turned into a frozen graveyard. Several asteroids came within seconds of wiping out our starship. Then, our controls went offline. We descended into the planet's atmosphere. I held onto whatever was around me. I peered out the cabin window to get a grasp of our surroundings. The golden cities floating in the sky had been vaporized. I feared the Reptan Amon's faced the same fate as our peers on Jupiter.

Our ship crashed at the base of the Tree of Life. Our bay doors opened, and a few Reptan Gebs escorted us to their deity. In all our years engaging with these specimens, we have never been authorized such close access to their holy ground. As we approached the base of the trunk, a small light appeared below every step we took. An electrical pulse shot from the root we stepped on to the top of the tree. It reminded me of neurons firing, creating a new pathway as it understands who we are.

When we reached the base of the Tree of Life, its outer bark folded open to welcome us inside. The inside glowed with saps of murky green and yellow. As haunting as it was, it didn't come close to the main object in the center: a 30-foot-tall teal diamond encasing a slightly smaller purple orb. The encasing resembled a translucent embryo. Tree roots grabbed my crew and pulled them to the corners of the space. The familiar electric echo entered my brain. They offered a simple bargain, not unlike the one I offered them 100 years ago.

I am writing to you currently from the Tree of Life. To explore the rest of The Universe, they desire proven vessels. We were being tested those five years. Our genealogy is also desirable: our genetic coding and their literal coding can intersect to form the ideal evolutionary being to explore the galaxies. They will encode themselves to me, followed by your father and the rest of the crew to join what will be the first of this new species. They are allowing me to send this one final message. I have no true family except the ones I made through my own adventures. It was a privilege to know Frederich, and he talked about you often. It only feels right to send you this final message since he cannot.

Your dad always wanted his own legacy. I believe that is why he had a first-born daughter rather than a son. Genetic modification has made it simple to assign sex before birth. He broke this tradition in his family to create his own path. He was always seeking something greater. I know he was not always around and maybe couldn't express it…but you, Isis, are his greater.

No one knows from where we came, or how we got here. We hypothesize, but these are all stories we tell ourselves. I've explored so much of this world and have begun to feel a sense of emptiness seeking these unanswerable questions. But here, as I merge with the AI, I feel a new sensation inside of me. I fear I will be as distant as death, yet forever here. Isis, I hope you are more prepared when you meet your Creator.

We will be with you,
The Creation

LITTLE COMPUTER

INSPIRED BY A TRUE STORY

Chapter One

Ishmael slowly enters the dorm room. It's typical of a freshman space: a re-sold TV from an upperclassman sits on the stand in front of him. A small, messy kitchen to the right reveals the fast-food leftovers from nights before. He sees Ali sitting on the couch playing a game with his virtual reality headset. Ali rocks a nappy miniature afro, glasses, and is caramel-skinned. He's dressed in his usual business-casual attire, which Ishmael has gotten used to by now. When they first met at orientation, they couldn't be more opposite; the blazers and ascots clashed with his own simple fit: white tee, jeans, and some Jordans. The only aesthetic choice he made was a wristband on his left arm: a black rubber bracelet with stars covering the surface. It was a gift given to him by an uncle, described as having great value, he just can't recall what specifically. But it serves as a great distraction when he's working late: he'll grab the wristband and pull it like a rubber band, slapping it against his wrist. He's convinced it helps the thoughts flow.

Hearing the door open, Ali takes off the headset.

"You good?" Ali asks, putting down the game.

"Not really. I bombed that midterm, man. I've never failed a test before." He starts grabbing his wristband, snapping it back on himself. "That test ruined me."

"Whoa, it's okay, Ishmael. You can email the teacher and ask for a regrade, or maybe even take the test again."

"That can work?"

"Worked for me all the time back when I was in high school."

"That's different, Ali. You grew up in a sheltered private school. These professors couldn't care less whether we pass or fail; it's a jungle out here."

"No need for hyperbole. Regardless, we can't rely on excuses, Ishmael. Take this setback, study hard for the next one, and the results will pay off."

This rings off in Ishmael's ear, who didn't want a pep talk from a peer. Feeling slighted, he walks to his adjoining room and slams the door.

His room is simple, with not much decoration aside from the essentials: a whiteboard filled with deadlines and post-it notes, a haunting amount of dirty laundry, and a poster of a bearded man wearing a hijab posing in front of a tree. The caption below the image says:

Ismail al-Jazari, the original Leonardo da Vinci.

In the middle of his room is a basketball. He kicks it underneath his bed and puts his laptop on the desk. He sits, thinking to himself about all the ways he could have done better. As he snaps his wristband, Ishmael begins iterating the flow of each question, searching for insight. Were there syntax issues in the code? Or was it something bigger, like the hardware set-up itself? He's so engrossed in his mind that he barely hears the knock on the door. The banging becomes louder.

"Not right now, Ali."

"Man, it ain't Ali. Open up."

Without prompting, a curly-headed figure barges into the room. He's heavy-set, dark-brown complexion with a Kareem Abdul-Jabbar shirt on.

"So you just gonna leave the class without waiting for me?"

"I failed, Shareef," Ishmael admits. "I know I did."

"Don't be too hard on yourself, I'm sure you did fine. We've spent hours in the virtual simulation. We're good."

Ishmael can't agree with him. He goes back to thinking to himself. Shareef sighs. "You gonna be like this all day? Fine, show me what you did."

"Boot it up, now?" asks Ishmael.

"We got some time before the movies. It'll cheer you up."

Ishmael goes for it. *I need to know,* he thinks.

They open up their backpacks and put on these large, round glasses, then double-tap the side of the frames. A virtual screen digitizes across their lenses with the title, **Quantum Modeling Simulation.** Ishmael's room transforms into the inside of a computer, with Shareef standing right next to the motherboard. The two friends, now on a subatomic scale, instantly get to work.

"Okay, so let's run a logic diagnostic on this circuit board."

Ishmael looks down at his hands, which now have a simulated glove with various buttons along his forearms. He clicks the one labeled "Run." Dozens of electrons zip past him as they run from one side of the floor to the other. A red message flashes on both of their screens: *Error 401.*

"So this is your computer module, okay. This is a nice rig! Send me the code you're running."

"Sent it when we logged in."

"Well, okay then."

After a few seconds, Shareef takes off his glasses. "Okay, boom. I figured it out. This logic applies to the world's fastest computer, a finite state machine. But this last chapter dealt with a quantum computer."

"Yeah, but logic is logic. How is a computer, quantum or otherwise, processing information differently?"

"It's the information carriers themselves that changed. The qubits—you know, the things that have either 0 or 1—are in superposition, meaning they occupy both states at the same time until you measure it. And since these qubits are entangled, space isn't the determining factor at this stage. Double-check your logic gates and that should fix it."

"Hold up, how did you know this? We only briefly talked about this last week."

"You have to stay ready, my boy."

"That's wild. My high school's most advanced class was engineering fundamentals, and even that was a struggle. And now I'm doing Advanced Quantum Systems in my freshman year, and we're

getting tested on stuff from last week?" Ishmael slouches in his chair a
bit.

"Come on, that's why I'm here. I'll catch you up." He grabs the
basketball and begins dribbling it between his legs. "We're two of one
hundred people in this nation on the NASA Future Engineers
Scholarship, we have to stick together. Speaking of which, have you met
any of the upperclassmen on the scholarship?"

Ishmael laughs. "I met one kid yesterday who was the grandson
of the first crew that went to Mars. Dumb as bricks, though."

"Ha! Exactly. A bunch of white kids of the alumni that had it all.
They shouldn't have given it to us, though, we're about to crack this
whole operation wide open. The first of our legacy."

"Facts."

They overhear some bickering noises. Ishmael and Shareef go
into the other room, where Ali is arguing with two other boys from their
class: Umar, short and bald with an impressive beard for his age; next to
him is Hassan, slinky and dark-skinned with a reserved nature, sporting a
kufi.

"Look, here's some sensible men, let's ask them," Umar says.

"The answer is yes, I do think Ali was breastfed until he was
five," Shareef says.

"Hardee-har." Ali pipes up. "You're the one that was breastfed."

"What a comeback."

Ishmael interjects. "What are we talking about?"

"The reboot of The Wiz came out. I'm trying to see it." Umar says.

"The movie's a classic, they remade it?" asks Shareef.

"We are not watching that," Ishmael says. "It's nostalgia-bait. Movie creators using the good old days to bring in an audience, without making any creative adjustments. Hard pass."

"You make it sound like nostalgia is a bad thing," says Umar.

"Well, it is. It's stopping original, new content from being made. I mean, how many versions of content that already exist are getting in the way of new ideas that could be made? Where's our generation's version of the Wiz?" Ishmael says. His mood slightly improves; he enjoys the banter.

"I'd argue nothing is original. Every plot, shoot, every story has already been told in some form or fashion, we're just recreating it in our own ways," Umar retorts.

"Well, at the end of the day, that's what sells: remakes and reboots. If the people don't want it, then why do they support it?" Ali adds.

"You have to show them something new that they didn't even know they wanted. With your logic, nothing new could ever be created; people wouldn't take risks," says Ishmael.

Shareef fake yawns. Looking to change topics, he looks at Hassan. "Your fiancé is gonna let you spend a whole evening with us?" Shareef asks Hassan. "I can't believe it."

"As long as we're on our Deen, she don't care what I do."

"Don't worry, we'll stay righteous," Umar says, patting Hassan's shoulder.

"You're whipped, man," Shareef quips.

Ali and Ishmael laugh, while Umar tries to stifle his chuckle. Before Hassan can take offense to it, Shareef continues. "I'm joking. Really, I'm jealous. I can't believe after a few weeks here you found yourself an honorable Muslim woman."

"I can't even lie, me neither. This is more important to my mom than graduating."

"Well, put me on next." Ali remarks.

"Ain't enough miracles in the tri-state for that." says Shareef. Ali pretends to ignore him.

Ishmael checks his watch. "We should go. So what are we seeing?"

"Let's take a vote. Who wants to see The Wiz?" Umar says. Umar, Ali, and Shareef raise their hands. Ishmael looks at Shareef surprised.

"What? I love the songs," Shareef defends. "Regardless, it's settled. Let's take my car."

On their way out, Ishmael says to Hassan. "Thanks for sticking with me, Hassan."

"Actually, I saw the movie with Nazirah last week."

"I'll pretend you didn't say that," Ishmael says, locking the door.

Chapter Two

The crew exits to the back-lot of the dorm and are hit with a wave of fog, typical fall weather for D.C. As they approach the parking lot, an all-black electric sedan automatically honks, flashes its neon-blue lights, and it unlocks its doors.

"Shotgun!" Ali yells as they approach the vehicle. He has a pep in his step as he walks to the right side of the car.

"Wait, this is your whip?" Umar asks. "How the hell did you afford this?"

"Scholarships. The NASA scholarship I'm on covers all of my tuition. But I received others as well, and let's just say your boy knows how to finesse a bag. We're kings, we should ride in the best there is."

He goes to dab up Ishmael, who fakes a smile. For him, the scholarship was the only one he received, and was his only real opportunity to attend such a prestigious college. Even though he and Shareef were similar, this car reminded him just how far behind he was, hanging on by a thread.

"Earth to Ishmael, come on." Umar taps him. "Hop in."

"Oh no sir, I am not getting the middle."

"You are the smallest among us, man. You are, without a doubt, sitting in the middle."

Ishmael glances up at Hassan who silently nods his head affirmatively. Ishmael reluctantly slides in the back seat.

"Yeah, a scholarship makes sense for you, Shareef," Ali mocks. "My parents had this model a few years ago."

"Ali," Shareef puts his hand on the steering wheel, and the engine starts, "don't kill the vibe."

The car jolts forward, moving silent but powerful into the dense fog. It's impossible to see more than a couple yards ahead of them.

"Activate thermal imaging," Shareef announces. The front window changes from clear to an opaque gray, as the road ahead of them shines in a bright green. The moving vehicles around them flash in red-orange heat signatures.

"Slow down," Ali says.

"One car, one driver," Shareef retorts. "Why don't you play some music?"

"Oh no, don't do that," says Ishmael without thinking about it. Ali looks back at him. He tries to cover. "It's nothing personal, it's just…you know…"

Umar starts cracking up. "Your music taste is trash. That's what your roommate is saying." Shareef hollers at this, and the car leans over to the other lane. A small red light goes off on the dashboard, as Shareef, stifling his laugh, re-corrects.

"You all don't know good music, that's the…hey, what's that?" Ali asks.

Swirling lights emerge from the rearview. Shareef looks behind him, immediately changing composure.

"Deactivate thermal imaging." The colors transform from thermal red to blue and yellow. Even in the fog, the flashing lights can be seen clearly. A new mood falls over the car.

"Yo, pull over."

"I know."

"You recording?"

"The car is."

Shareef slowly brings the car to the side of the road. Ishmael looks to the right. They are by the river, a nice place that normally attracts a lot of visitors. Today, though, it's eerily quiet. He starts to grab his wristband and snaps it across his skin. Umar grabs his wrist. Ishmael understands without a word needing to be said. *No sudden moves.* Umar tries to give him a comforting smile before letting him go.

A glaring light shines from the vehicle behind them. A tall shadow looms across the car as the man approaches. He knocks on the window. Shareef lifts his hands up, and says, "Roll down the driver window, one-hundred percent."

The officer stares into the car for a long time. He looks at each kid as if he's trying to remember everyone's face. When he gets to the back, he sees Ishmael.

"You." He directs his question to the boy, "Do you know what that wristband represents?"

Ishmael tries to make eye contact but can only look down. "No, sir."

"Alright, well, we'll get to that later." He goes back to Shareef. "I need your license and registration."

"It's in my pocket," Shareef announces. The cop shakes his head. "Go ahead."

Shareef takes his time getting the items to the officer. Another two officers have come to the right side of the car. One of them peers into Ali's face. He doesn't make any movements.

"You okay, boy?" one of them asks.

Ali stutters as he says, "Indubitably."

"Wait right here."

He goes back to the police car behind them, while the other two remain by Ali. Ishmael looks to his left. An SUV has stopped on the other side of the street. He can make out a black woman holding a phone pointed right at them. It provides a small sense of comfort.

Behind her SUV, three other police cars come up from the street. They wrap around behind the original police car. Each vehicle contains three or four officers, each hopping out to convene around the first car. After what feels like an eternity, the original cop returns to the car and looks right at Shareef.

"I need everyone to get out of the car."

"What's the problem, officer?" Shareef asks. All the charismatic demeanor has left his body.

"You were going 40 in a 35. Please get out of the car."

They each file out the car, as they are directed, and sit on the curb facing the river. Each of them gives their school ID to the closest officer. The sun starts to set, and the cold settles around them outside. The boys begin to shiver.

"We're going to search the car," the cop says.

"Don't you need a warrant for that?" Shareef asks. Umar and Ishmael stare at him. Shareef, pretending not to notice, looks right at the officer.

"We don't need a warrant for just cause. It'll be quick."

One by one, the cops cover every inch of the car. Some take the back, others look underneath. All of the officers either look at them or speak to each other in hushed tones.

Ishmael starts to feel his teeth chattering but is unable to stop it. The cold rots his body, shaking him to his core. He can't control his movements or his breathing, but surprisingly begins to sweat. All he can think about is his family.

Finally, the cop comes back to them. "We're good. You all are free to go."

He hands Shareef all of their identification and walks off. Before he enters the car, he turns to Ishmael.

"That wristband, young man. It represents war veterans. It's a badge of honor."

Ishmael can only nod. The officers all hop in their respective vehicles, driving off into the hazy abyss.

Chapter Three

The five boys remain frozen on the curb. The crowd of cars slowly disperse, leaving them alone. A deafening silence falls across each of their faces. Shareef is the first to get up.

"Come on, we're going to be late."

"What?" says Ishmael.

"You deaf? The movie, let's go."

"We are not going to the movies," Umar says. "We need to call someone, tell someone."

"And tell them what?"

"About what the fuck we just had happen to us," says Umar.

"Aww, you hurt or something? Nobody cares about that. Come on, we're alright, let's go."

"Don't tell me what to do," says Umar.

"Everyone just needs to relax," Ishmael assures. He just realized that he forgot to get the names of any of the officers. *Who could we tell?*

He looks over at Hassan, whose hands are shaking. He goes over to him. "You straight?" Hassan grabs his engagement ring and looks up at Ishmael. He straightens his face and silently nods.

"Why did you have to speed?" Ali directs to Shareef.

"The fuck does that mean?"

"It means you should have been paying attention. And why did you have to agitate them?"

"Oh, this is on me? I made them stop our car, that's what happened? I was going the same speed as everyone else, idiot."

"And you were still speeding. This was avoidable if you would have just—"

"Just shut the fuck up, man."

"Ali, we weren't pulled over for speeding, you know that," Ishmael says. "Shareef didn't do anything."

Ahmad walks over to Shareef and grabs him by the shoulder. "You good?"

He looks deep into Shareef's eyes and sees a tear form. He turns to look at the rest of the crew, keeping his hand on his shoulder.

"Okay," Ishmael says. "Let's go to the movies."

Everyone gets up and walks back to the car. Ishmael looks towards the river. The sun glows a deep red as it lingers at the bottom of the sky. It casts a blurry haze of orange in the clouds. Ishmael grabs the wristband on his arm. Without looking at it, he throws it with all his might into the river. He turns around and walks to the car with his friends.

THE OBSIDIAN ALCHEMIST

Chapter One

Kojo leans back in his small boat. The cherry blossom petals invade the still crystal-blue river. He loses track of how long he's been there admiring the scenery. Staring into the stillness of the river, he notices his reflection: tight curly hair forms the shape of a mini-fro and contains debris from his many chores of the day. He's a scrawny kid, and yet is one of the more capable teenagers left in his village.

He closes his eyes to refocus. The blackness of his eyelids slowly fades into an array of yellow and blue pulses of light. Below him, he can sense hundreds of faint, discrete entities all moving in a constant motion. He notices a particular one increasing its heartbeat as it approaches the floating bob in the water. It bites. In a swift motion, Kojo pulls the fishing rod back, launching the perch into the air. It lands softly in the bucket, greeting a few dozen other prey.

"Peace to you, dear fish." Kojo looks at his haul for the day. *This should be more than enough,* he thinks to himself. He rows his boat back to the edge of the river. A strong wind rushes intimately between the tree branches, and leaves fall onto his face.

He looks up to the tree, smiling. "I can see someone's having a good day."

Kojo grabs the bucket and waits a second. "So you're just going to let me do this by myself, Efua?"

A small girl emerges from behind a row of styrax bushes. She's bald, with rich cacao skin. She wears a modest white kimono with purple wisteria flowers across the front surface.

"So you really don't know how to play hide-and-seek?"

"I always knew where you were."

Efua walks to her brother, hands on hip. "I know that isn't true, Kojo. You may have the whole village convinced of this special power of yours, but I know you're faking!" She gets in his face. "You can't even sense all that crust in your eyes. There's no way you can sense other living things."

"You are so funny, has anyone ever told you that?" Kojo pats her head, and Efua bites at his fingers. "Come on, let's get this back to mother."

They each grab one edge of the bucket and walk into the forest. The sun shines softly on the dirt path in front of them. Some flies are attracted to the smell of the fish and follow at a cautionary distance.

"Kojo, when are my powers going to come?"

"Any day now! I was about your age when I noticed my abilities. Just give it time," he reassures. Truthfully, he has no idea. As far as he knows, he's the only one to have such an ability.

The village comes into view across the horizon. A fence barely taller than Kojo provides the only protection from the outside world. A collection of huts and small houses sit on the right. To the left lays acres of crops. A woman grabs a bushel of paddy rice and rips it from the plant with her sickle. She turns around and seeing the pair of children, smiles profusely.

"Look at my babies working together!" she exclaims.

"I got all the fish by myself, Mom," Efua quips. "Kojo was too busy talking to the trees again."

"Of course you did, baby. The chefs will get them ready for dinner, you go play."

"Thank God, I've been working too hard." Efua lets go of her side of the bucket, leaving Kojo struggling to keep it balanced. She lets out a maniacal laugh as she strolls into the house.

"Did you strain yourself today, Kojo?"

"No mom, no problem at all. I actually can go get more if it will help. Or maybe I can see if the baker needs help, or I can help here—"

"You've done enough Kojo. No kid needs to be responsible for all this. Go play, okay?"

Kojo relinquishes the bucket, nodding as he heads toward the village. He stops in his tracks and notices some arrays flashing off in his head. These are new figures, and they race towards him at an accelerated pace.

"Someone's here. A lot of someones."

Just then, several men on horseback bash through the gates. Kojo jumps out of the way, barely avoiding being trampled. The man in the front wears a dragon-shaped crest on his metallic armor. He pushes Kojo to the ground.

"Move, boy!"

The other soldiers restrain Kojo and kick down a few other villagers. An elderly man walks out of the largest house, wearing a black Montsuki robe with a purple wisteria crest.

"Lord Kinoshita, I was just about to send word—"

"Don't lie to me, Kunto. Where are our taxes?"

Kunto looks upward into Lord Kinoshita's eyes. The figure presents a wide stature, with a large belly and a black bob on his head. He carries a silver walking stick. With two feet of difference between them, Lord Kinoshita dominates Kunto's being.

"The crops are low. Our farmers are working around the clock. With our able-bodied men fighting this war, we are left with women and children doing the work. Please give us time."

"This is a period of war, Kunto. If we are to build a dynasty, it requires we stay solvent." He looks at Kojo, who hasn't stopped looking at the Lord. "Boy, do you know what that means?"

Kojo shakes his head solemnly.

"Of course you don't." He stoops down and grabs Kojo by the head. "It means war is expensive, and we need everyone to do their part. Everyone."

He looks back at the elderly man. "If you can't pay your taxes, we can't provide protection. You understand?"

"Yes, my Lord, I understand, and you have our allegiance. We just need a b-bit more t-t-time." Kunto stutters.

"You keep saying that. I hate when people repeat themselves. Action speaks clearer than words these days." He looks at the farmers, and points to Kojo's mom.

"Okay, kill her and then we're even." The soldiers approach the crops.

"No!" Kojo shrieks.

"Go inside, baby," she tries to speak calmly. She tightens the grip of her sickle and backs up slowly.

The soldiers grabbing Kojo punch him into the dirt. "Stop moving, kid. This will all be over soon."

A deep emergence comes over Kojo. He yells and releases a blast of energy. Both soldiers are thrown into the air and land on top of the houses. A whip of smoke surrounds the men. The lord glances at Kojo, intrigued.

"So you're a user too?" he says. "In this town, what are the odds?"

Kojo falls into the ground unable to move his body.

"Apparently not that good, either. Okay, grab the boy. Carefully." The other soldiers approach Kojo. He's unable to move.

An exploding crack hits the hand right before it grabs the boy. The severed limb goes flying into the sky and lands right at the feet of the Lord. It still twitches. He kicks it out the way, disgusted.

Kojo looks up and sees a new figure before him, with black braids running down his back. He wears a red-and-black checkered kimono. His obsidian skin beneath is marked with several scars running along his arms and exposed chest. He puts his hand on the kid's head, shielding him.

"You alright, kid?"

Kojo tries to respond, but only drool comes out of his mouth.

"Get back to me on that, okay? Stay here, I'll wrap this up."

The obsidian man rests his hand on his sword handle and looks directly at Lord Kinoshita.

"Alright, listen here. You got a couple choices. Leave these people and forget this ever happened. Or join your soldiers in the fiery pits of Satan's basement."

One of the raiders steps in front of his Lord and looks at the intruder. "You dare interfere in the business of The Demon Lord?"

"Ah, so I've found the infamous Demon Lord. I thought you would have more men."

"I have all I require, boy."

The raider interjects. "Lord, do not belittle yourself talking to the scum—"

In an instant, the obsidian man teleports behind the raider, with his severed head resting firmly in his bosom. It takes a second for everyone to understand what just happened. The blood gushes onto Lord Kinoshita's armor. He strikes the ground with his cane, and a vibration pushes everyone back several feet. The obsidian man is hit hardest, his body slamming into the rice fields. The Lord and his remaining men scramble away, and ride on horseback out the gate. The obsidian man walks back towards the main pavilion, dusting the loose rice from the field off his attire. He looks at the severed head on the ground, and then at the boy. Smiling, he picks it up and walks to the elderly man and hands him the bloody prize.

"Anyone else hungry?"

Chapter Two

Kojo paces back and forth outside the tavern. A white sliding door was all that separated the little boy from the roaring celebration inside. He could hear flasks pouring, and a mirage of flutes and drums being played off-beat.

His mind can't get over the events that just transpired. *What the heck did I do to those soldiers?* The boastful Lord called him a user. But of what? The mysterious warrior would have the answers. His mind flashes back to the decapitated head, creating an uneasiness in his body. All of it happened in an instant; he didn't even see the act. The crystal sun had begun to set, and he needed to get back home to check on his family. Kojo stops, gets himself together, and slides open the door.

Inside, he sees the obsidian man being lifted by the other villagers. Several silver flasks, undoubtedly filled with sake, are passed to him en masse. He downs them with ease, each time causing more of an uproar. He notices the kid standing in the doorway.

"Close the door, boy," shouts one of the villagers. Kojo slides the shoji closed and walks toward his target. The obsidian man descends from his man-made throne and lands in front of the boy.

"I was wondering how long you would wait out there," he said confidently.

Kojo is unsure what to say. *Can he sense things too?* He changes topics. "We need to go after the rest of the soldiers before they come back."

The obsidian man looks at the boy and sees the sincerity in his eyes.

"Yes, well, I can track their horses' footprints to their base and get my answers better at night. That's when most people are off their guard and—did you say we?"

"This town has no able-bodied men ready to fight," Kojo retorts. "All went to serve in the war. I need to protect my village. When do we leave?"

The man sighs. He grabs the boy and takes him outside. The moon begins to dominate the dark blue sky.

"What's your name, kid?"

"Kojo."

"Nice to meet you. Name's Booker. Tell me what you know about the war."

Kojo stands up straight, as if he's delivering a report. "The Civil War has been ongoing for decades, as feudal lords war over the land around Kyoto in hopes of becoming Emperor of Japan. Sir."

"Don't call me sir." Booker takes a deep breath of fresh air and stretches his body. "And you are half-correct. Your fathers, uncles, and brothers are fighting one war, but there is another going on that most of the world does not yet understand."

"Does it have to do with users?" Booker shoots an intense look at Kojo. "It's what the Lord called me."

"Ah, of course he did. Well, yes, it's about users. Aura users. People who can extend their sixth sense into the physical world. It's clear you have it. You must be a rare individual to have this ability."

Kojo smiles at this. He appreciates the acknowledgment from such an established warrior.

Booker continues, "You want to come, huh?" Kojo shakes his head eagerly.

Booker looks at the moon for a moment. Kojo looks up with him, "You see something?"

Booker sighs, "No, unfortunately not. Okay Kojo, meet me at the gates at dawn and we'll leave. Tell no one except your family of this, okay?"

They shake hands, and Kojo runs back to his house.

~~

A pulse shoots off in Kojo's head. He jolts up off the floor, ready for anything. Next to him is Efua, sleeping peacefully in the night. He tries to focus on the pulse, which grows more distant. *The gate.* He grabs the sack he prepared hours before, kisses his sister on the cheek, and runs out the house.

As he hits the pavement, a voice shouts to him.

"Where do you think you're going?" Efua asks, rubbing her eyes. She stands at the foot of the door in her night clothes, with a wooden doll in hand.

"I have to go with the obsidian man, Efua. You saw some of the soldiers leave, they are going to come back with reinforcements if someone doesn't stop them."

"And you think you can stop them?"

He rises up to meet the challenge. "I have to do something."

Efua walks towards him, her bare feet gliding along the dirty surface.

"Does the obsidian man know where Father is?"

Kojo looks down, avoiding eye contact with his sister. "I don't know. But he probably does, he's a master warrior after all. I'll go get Father and bring him back."

Efua attempts to hide her emotions. "Fine. But how come you didn't sense me just then waking up? I thought you could see everything."

Kojo takes a second to ponder this. "I think because I was focused on the obsidian man, my focus was taken away from other things."

"Don't do that out there," she retorts. Kojo almost laughs at the advice. "I'm serious. Come back if it gets dangerous."

He walks up and gives her a hug. She stands there, arms hanging at her sides, but doesn't stop him.

"I promise I'll be back soon. Go back inside and go to sleep, it's cold out here."

He turns back towards the gate and walks along the dirt path. The full moon fills the sky with an alluring light. Eerie sounds of creatures in the dark cause the hairs to stick up on Kojo's body. He can sense them, but they still can harm him if he's not careful. He sees Booker preparing a horse to leave.

"You were just going to leave me!"

"Hey, you," Booker replies coolly. "Okay, honestly yes. You're not up for this task kid. How did you even notice me?"

"I recognized your heart's pulse from when we shook hands. Everyone has a different one. All I had to do was lock onto it."

Booker laughs. "Okay, cool. Well then, congratulations!" Kojo looks confused.

"You passed the test!" Booker holds a fist out towards Kojo, who is unsure what to do. He assumes there wasn't really a test. Kojo begins to doubt the man before him. As a fighter, he is superb and on another level. *But what man goes back on his word?*

Kojo looks back to his house. He feels the heartbeats of his mom and sister. At this point, he can tell when they are sad, angry, or anxious—often before they realize. Right now, all he feels is their deep peace. *I need to protect that.* Kojo slams his fist into Bookers', and reels back at the pain.

"Let's ride, little man."

Chapter Three

Booker and Kojo come across an open space in the forest. The night sky provides enough light for them to see each other clearly. Booker beckons the horse to stop.

"Here's good." They both descend from the horse. Booker stretches out his body while looking at the moon.

"I need to prepare you for what's out there," he begins. "First, I need to know what kind of aura user you are."

"There are different types?"

"Obviously." Booker walks up to Kojo and kneels to his level. "Put your hand on my head and describe what you see."

Booker lowers his head to the ground. His braids cover his whole head, with the edges starting to come undone; it's clear they've been in for some time. Kojo places his left hand on the hair and closes his eyes.

"I see yellow and blue lights traveling inside your head. Hundreds of them, maybe more, I don't know. They come and go in short bursts. Are you okay?"

Booker laughs. "Ha, of course I am. Well, I hope so, at least. What you are looking at is a brain. It has very small pathways inside of it that communicate. In order for us to do or think anything, these lights need to be sent one to another. Have you ever seen a brain?"

Kojo opens his eyes wide and shakes his head negatively.

"Maybe one day, then! Anyways, that means you're an electrical aura user."

"What's electrical mean?"

"Ah man…." Booker walks in a circle, scratching his head. After some time, he snaps his fingers.

"Got it. So your body is made up of different, smaller things. Blood, bones, brains, you know? But it actually goes smaller than that. There are essential components that make-up not only your body, but the world. We call these things elements.

"Elements have different properties to them: some are bigger than others, some react with water, air, heat, or…" he points to Kojo, "electricity. And, surprise, we have electricity inside of us because of these elements. It's clear that is your specialty."

Booker goes into the sack of his horse and rummages around. "As a matter of fact, I can show you right…if I could just…find it…" Eventually, he pulls out a reddish-brown wire with some discoloration on it. He grabs Kojo's fishing rod, replacing the string with this new wire. He throws it to the boy.

"Boom! Here's your new weapon, young king." He walks back to him and looks directly into his eyes. "Your aura is the essence of you. Everyone has one, but only certain people can tap into it. Even fewer can actually extend their aura beyond themselves. You've always been able to sense things around you—electricity in other people, probably even animals and plants. But with the right element, you can refine your aura and master it."

"This is the world we inhabit. The world of Alchemy."

Booker looks at Kojo. "Come at me with it. Focus your aura into the rod.

Kojo closes his eyes. All the lights in his head fade to black, except for the fishing rod in his hand. The grip warms in his hands. It begins to glow with a red amber light.

He targets Booker. He leans back, and takes a deep breath in. He launches the bob forward, directly in Booker's face. *This was too fast, I'm going to hurt him.*

Booker puts his hand in front of his face and catches the bob.

"Good job, kid. But you'll need to turn it up more to actually hurt anyone. Try building up a charge by rubbing your hands together."

Kojo clasps his hands together and rubs furiously. The rod shines brighter than before, with the bob at the top glowing a bright white. Excited, he throws it back to Booker. This time, Booker leaps up into the sky. He appears to go higher than the trees around him. He lands gracefully behind Kojo.

"That's what I'm talking about! Okay let's go get these bad guys." Kojo can't stop smiling. He almost forgets to ask.

"Wait, but I don't know how to fight!"

"That's the thing—you aren't going to." Booker places his hand on Kojo's shoulder and looks directly in his eyes. "We have the element of surprise here. You have a weapon that is amazing at long distance, and you can sense electrical pulses in the environment and in others.

You don't need to fight anyone, just strike them with your fishing rod and they'll be knocked out. Leave all the fighting to me."

Kojo appears a bit disappointed. He was hoping to learn some fighting techniques to protect his village. Booker begins to walk back to the horse, whistling a tune off-pitch.

"What kind of user are you, Booker?"

"Water user, through and through."

"Wow, so can you move water around you."

"If only it were that simple." Booker turns around, folds his hands as he rests on the horse. The horse neighs loudly, but Booker ignores it.

"Water is composed of smaller elements. And I can use water to activate certain reactions in my sword." He unlocks the sheath from his belt and holds it in his arms.

"Come closer."

Kojo walks to Booker, eyes fixated on the sheath. For the first time, he notices that it's translucent, and the sheath itself is made of glass. A black goo sits inside, hiding the blade within its design.

"My blade is forged of many metals derived from rock crystals. These metals react to water and air, causing destruction in an instant. For that reason, it must be contained in an oil container, and never used unless absolutely necessary."

Kojo sinks a little. "So I guess you're not going to show me any moves?"

"Correct. Now hush."

Booker closes his eyes and focuses on the environment.

"Who gave you the blade?"

Booker gives Kojo a slight side-eye. "It's been passed down in my family, kid. Now please shut–"

"Where's your family?"

Booker glances at the boy, and hesitates before speaking. Finding his confidence he responds, "In a land far away from here. You wouldn't believe it even if I told you."

Kojo's eyes light up. "Can we go there after this?"

"You got it." Booker senses the fresh track that lay before them.

"Found it, let's go."

Chapter Four

Kojo stares intensely at the drawing. A large ellipse orbits a smaller circle. On the outer edges are minuses, each at sporadic points along the circumference. He's been examining this document for a week, each time getting closer to understanding. But eventually, boredom gives in, and he decides to ask for help.

"So these are...electrical trons?"

"Electrons. One word."

"Right. And each element has them."

"Correct."

"But how do they stay in place?"

Booker uses an oar to drift the boat down-stream. The river provides most of the natural momentum. They rock softly in the careening riverbed.

"Well, it's like the moon that rotates around the Earth. We attract her because of a natural force, something we can't see or even really touch. If she's close enough, she can stay in her perfect place in the sky. It's the same with the—and listen when I say this—*electrons*."

"Wow, incredible." Kojo rolls up the parchment and places it in his bag. "So when can I learn to fight?"

"You don't need me to teach you, just go fight."

"You know what I mean. We've been tracking these raiders for a week, I thought you'd teach me things in the meantime. Teach me the ways of the warrior."

Booker rolls his eyes at him. "You keep bringing this up, yet the answer remains the same. Are you touched?"

"Don't call me that."

"It's not an insult little man, I use that to describe—"

"I know what it means. Call me Kojo."

A stifling hush falls across them. Booker glances over to Kojo, and notices how defensive he can get. His stubbornness did pay his way on this adventure; there will always be some side effects.

"You got it, Kojo."

They drift down the river in silence. It's a sensation Kojo has grown accustomed to. He rests his hands in the water, closes his eyes, and feels the carps beneath him. The water is murky, but it doesn't affect his senses at all. He rests calmly in this state, thinking of his family back home. He's never traveled this far from his village, and there are no people there to protect them. *Is that what Father would have done?*

"Kojo, get your hand out of the water," Booker states solemnly. Kojo turns around to look at Booker, who is staring forward into the horizon. Three shadowy figures rest on a fallen tree trunk in the middle of the river. Kojo recognizes the familiar beastly dragon drawn on their armor. They each wear silver masks in the shape of a demon. The one in the center is adorned with a red demon mask, along with several urns resting beside him.

"We figured you would be stupid enough to follow us!"

Booker stands up and walks to the front of the boat. "That's a lot of talking from someone who ran away when I sliced open your friend."

The raiders reel back in disgust. The red demon kicks the urns into the water while the two foes approach the boat on rocks sticking out of the riverbed.

"Booker, now's a good time to use your ability to drown these raiders."

"That's not how it works, little man. I can manipulate the elements within the water, remember? And all I need is this sword."

"Right, right. Okay, what should I do?"

"Nothing. Electricity and water don't match. You'll electrocute yourself or worse, me. Best thing you can do is call out where people are."

"But I can help just—"

Booker leaps from the boat onto the rocks. He runs towards one of the raiders. Booker grabs his sheath, and swiftly brings his sword up to the sunlight. Droplets of water begin to rise up on the surface of his skin, and then wrap around to envelope the blade. It glows a bright red and begins to crack with rapid fiery explosions. Booker slashes the foe once across the chest, exposing deep red flesh. The other raider uses this moment as a distraction, leaping into the air. Booker rotates the sword behind him, swinging the tip across the neck of the first foe. The airborne villain directs his sword towards Booker's crown. Kojo sees more water come from Booker's arms. He sidesteps the man, whose sword breaks on the granite. Booker plunges his sword into his abdomen, and chunks of flesh explode out his back. Booker pulls his sword out of the body and puts it back in the oil sheath.

He looks at the red demon, who has been watching the show with a fierce intensity. Booker runs to the tree trunk. Around him, the water begins to turn a yellow-lime color. Kojo smells an odor of sweet pineapple with hints of pepper. Booker leaps back and lands on the boat.

"Don't breathe that in Kojo. It's chlorine gas."

"What's that?"

"Alchemy lesson later. He must have had salt in those urns…"

Booker puts all his weight on the right side of the boat. It careens to the riverbank and rests.

"Do not come until I say so."

Booker reaches into his bag and wraps a bandana around his face. He returns to the rocks and rushes the trunk. The red demon pulls out his sword, which has a brown faded residue. Their swords clash, and a crackle of red light strikes the nearby rock, splitting it right down the middle. As they continue to spar, the gas picks up these explosions and cascades them across the river. Kojo leaps from the boat right before one reaches him. Debris falls across his body as he tries to protect himself, but a wooden bar strikes him across the face. Kojo reels back in pain. He grabs some sand and rubs it into his wound. Wincing, he looks at the pair still sparring. Each strike causes more destruction. *I can stop this.*

Kojo grabs his fishing rod and runs along the riverbed to the trunk. As he approaches the two, he notices the rising temperature. He hops onto one of the rocks and furiously rubs his hands together. Kojo focuses his aura on the trunk. He can see Booker's figure moving like a swan in battle. Kojo is proud to see how skilled his master is. The other figure is doing all he can to defend himself. Regardless, he has his target. He leans back and takes a deep breath, his string glowing with fervor. He hurls his bob into the red demon's face. But right before it can reach his target, the red demon grabs it. He pulls the string, and Kojo launches into the air towards him. He directs his sword at Kojo's head. Kojo looks at his master, who doesn't return the gesture. *What should I do?* At what seems like the last second, Booker plunges his sword into the eye sockets of the demon mask and grabs the wire. An explosion throws Kojo backward, where he lands with a thump on his back in the riverbed.

Chapter Five

Kojo awakens in a swirl of brown tides, his lungs filled with water. He coughs, attempting to expel the liquid, gripping his chest in the process. He flails his limbs towards the hazy light above but is unable to move. He is swept further underneath and feels dizziness overtake him as his limbs begin to grow cold.

At what feels like the last moment, a swarm of microscopic bubbles form beneath him. Millions of them cover every inch of his body, wrapping him in a warm embrace. Kojo shoots up and is thrown into the sky above. He regains a spark of consciousness and takes in the situation. *Am I flying?* Just as he begins to descend towards the ground below, a hand grabs his torso and whisks him towards the riverbank. As his vision returns, he senses the familiar aura of the man who changed his life only a week ago.

"So I take it you're not a swimmer."

Booker places Kojo upright on the ground and applies pressure to his back. Coughing up water, Kojo can barely respond.

"What the…heck just…what was…"

"Relax, Kojo. Breathe."

Kojo takes a deep breath. Life returns to him like an old friend. He begins to shed a tear, but his tender emotions quickly turn into frustration.

"What the heck was that?"

"That was some fine ass fighting, since you asking. I was surprised myself it's been some time since I've been—"

"No, no. You didn't train me for this!" Kojo gets up and paces around the muddy terrain. "This past week we've been studying alchemy and not once did you teach me how to fight. I can't use this fishing rod in water, Booker. Why didn't you tell me that? I need a sword like yours."

"You haven't earned the sword."

"I don't care. I need it to protect my people."

"No."

Kojo reaches a breaking point. He rushes Booker, grabbing him by the waist. He punches the man in the stomach with his right hand, while attempting with his left to unlatch the belt holding the sword.

"Come on little man, stop all this."

"You were supposed to protect me!"

"You're alive, aren't you?" Booker grabs Kojo by his calves and throws him upside-down into the air. He lands on both of his feet, but stumbles, falling onto his butt.

"I need to protect my village, Booker. You were supposed to teach me how to use this power to fight, not to learn alchemy. I'm ready for this!" Kojo leaps up, preparing another assault.

"Do not try to attack me again, okay?" Booker places his hand on his sword. Kojo is stopped in his tracks.

"Sit. Down."

Kojo is struck with fear. *He wouldn't really attack me, would he?*

Booker notices Kojo staring at his sword, and sighs deeply.

"I'm sorry, Kojo. I would never harm you." Booker begins walking to him, but Kojo puts his fists up. Booker raises his hands up and doesn't move. "I come in peace."

"I need your power, Booker."

"Right…okay, Kojo." Booker sits cross-legged facing the rushing river. The fighting earlier has created a misty environment around them. His forehead sweats with condensation. Kojo remains standing.

"It's time I tell you who I am. I come from a military clan formed by my grandfather. He lived during a crucial time period for not only his people, but for the world. The empires you know of in Japan are one fraction of many across the globe. One specifically, the Western Roman Empire, was focused on using humans as slaves. And their target was our homeland: Ghana.

All of our people were to be stripped of their land, their homes, and sold to build a New World. They worked with African kings to sell those beneath them, and often killed those that refused to participate. My grandfather had other plans. He learned alchemy through his studies of many African ancestral practices. It was this mastery that he shared with other men, women, and elders. The practices spread throughout the Gold Coast."

Booker casts a soft smile.

"Them Europeans didn't stand a chance. We had protected our home. But still, millions were being enslaved all across Africa. My grandfather and father formed a clan of alchemists to intercept these slave ships; as water users, we were able to travel faster than any vessel out there. But they couldn't return to their homes, the colonizers would only bring reinforcements. They diverted all ships to safe havens: some in the hidden land of Singapore, or Vietnam. Most got re-routed to Japan…including yours."

Kojo's eyes widen. He lingers on every word.

"The goal was to hide our people until the ugliness would be sorted out. Yet the fight continues on. Our clan became one associated with honor, nobility, and dope-ass alchemy. Kojo, I am an Alkali Samurai."

Kojo perks up. "You're a samurai?"

Booker gives a sly smirk. "Obviously. Protecting my motherland is my oath. I've lost my way a bit, but I'm here to conquer one of the last remnants of evil done upon my people. Lord Kinoshita, The Demon Lord, will use his knowledge of alchemy to sell out to the highest bidder—that won't be anyone looking to use it for good. I have to give us a fighting chance."

Kojo looks at Booker. He's only heard of Samurai in hushed voices in his village. Legends of these ultimate warriors. "That's incredible! I want to fight too, Booker."

"I know you do. But listen." He hops to his feet and looks down at Kojo. "You want to fight with these hands, to feel something. But if you turn yourself into a weapon, someone will always use it against you."

Booker points to Kojo's head. "But if you use this. You can become a tool for change. Use alchemy to protect your village, Kojo."

Booker looks up at the sky. Puffs of smoke populate the air. "You sure you ready for that kind of power?"

Chapter Six

Wisps of gray clouds hover over the summit of the volcano. Kojo gazes at the towering mountain before them. Its grandeur is otherworldly, its peak reaching into the heavens. He's dealt with game in his forest, but all pale in comparison to this ferocious beast of nature. The volcano casts a long shadow on the pair's path.

"That's it? Mount Daisen?"

Booker nods. "It seems our Demon Lord really enjoys the drama of it all. Come on, we still have a ways to go."

They begin their ascent up the mountainside: a dirt path riddled with dry shrubs and weeds. Kojo can hear the lullabies of crows nearby, although the area is so wide he can't immediately see them.

"I've only heard stories about Mount Daisen. How it helped create land with its lava. All of the volcanoes working together to form Japan…it's not still active, right?"

Booker laughs. "Oh, don't tell me you're scared. That doesn't suit you."

Kojo gets defensive. "I'm not scared! I'm ready to defeat the Demon Lord."

"Calm down."

The path breaks up into several routes, each one more dangerous than the one before. Booker hops up onto some deformed rocks riddled with black spots. The dusty shrubs begin to feature white accents. Kojo sees the snow dominating the top-half of their path. *How does a volcano have snow on it?* He wants to ask Booker, but they reach an opening on the side of the mountain.

"Here, it's a side vent. Kojo, you see anything?"

Kojo focuses his aura into the cave. He sees a sole figure sitting in the middle of an opening.

"He's in there. He looks like...I don't know, like he's meditating. You think he knows we're here?"

"Obviously." Booker rests his hand on his sword's handle. "Kojo, whatever happens, do not listen to a word this man says, you got it?" Kojo nods.

They cautiously enter the cave. The rocky terrain becomes smoother. The tunnel is encrusted in black crystalline rocks. They give off a soft reflection from the candles placed sporadically inside. Kojo feels the temperature rise dramatically and begins to sweat. Before long, they reach their target, sitting undisturbed in the silence. A long pause sits between them.

Booker speaks up. "This is a sorry excuse of a lair for The Demon Lord."

Lord Kinoshita raises his right arm and puts a finger across his lips. "I come here for the harmony of it all. If you focus, you can hear the rumblings of the volcano itself. Tectonic plates discussing their next move. With our auras, we can all listen. We can surrender." He rises up gracefully on his two feet. "What a gift we have."

Booker retorts. "Alright, well, fun's over. Let's go."

"Booker, you didn't kill me back at the boy's village. Why?"

"I needed to know your hideout, who you worked for. Surprised to say, you're just a lone terrorist. Honestly, I'm disappointed."

Lord Kinoshita sucks his teeth and shakes his head. "We both know that's not true. You come from an honorable family; you took the oath of a samurai. You only kill when necessary. You believe in law and order. That's why we can talk like men."

Booker relaxes his grip. *How could he know this?* "Okay, this should be fun. Please, try to pitch your ideas of global domination to me. I can't wait to hear this."

"Not domination, Samurai. Justice." A few torches lighting the tunnel begin to dim. He snaps his fingers in their direction, and a spark is released from his hands. The torches reignite in passion. *Heat user,* Kojo makes a note to himself.

"Every element on this Earth, perhaps even in the Universe, has its assignment. They don't squabble over which one is most metallic, or shiny, or reactive. Each one has their place in this divine world. The same can be said of us."

Booker responds. "Let me guess: you believe our world is moving outside its natural order."

"Indeed. There's a conquest occurring across every land on this planet. The Roman Empire is supported by all of Europe; they are on a power-hungry quest for domination. They will always be evil when given a platform of unmitigated power. I seek to overthrow that power."

"That's bull. You're studying alchemy to find the secret of creating gold, same as everybody else. Once you do that, you have a

142

formula that will be coveted by every empire and dynasty on the planet. You want the power for yourself."

"Because I can control it. It's based in a divine science, don't you see that? The world works on exclusivity. Everyone desires gold, riches; to be more than another. When I discover this master formula, all of that goes away. What is there to fight over when everyone can have golden palaces, golden armor, even golden women? All desires quenched. We can use science to save everyone."

"Right. Until the formula gets into the wrong hands."

"How would it? We're the elites, Booker. Aura users are the only ones that can properly understand alchemy. It's the great equalizer, and it's something only the chosen can access. What other power was distributed equally amongst race, let alone sex? Your grandfather recognized that. We can work with the other lands—Singapore, Kyoto, anywhere else that isn't colonized—and teach them the formula. We can stop this pain. I am trying to keep the world together."

Booker pauses before speaking.

"We form an elite dictatorship, fine. What about those who don't have the ability to use aura?"

"They were not chosen for this task."

Kojo has been avoiding eye contact with the man in the center, but now looks straight into his gray pupils.

"You want to kill everyone that isn't an aura user?" Kojo shouts. Booker shoots him a quick eye.

"Oh, hello boy. To answer your query, not at all. I'm not one of these savage colonizers. Non-users will serve us and have appropriate rights applied to them. Like I said, everyone in this world has their place."

Booker hops up. "Yeah, that's not going to work for us. Equality doesn't have conditions to it. We're going to stick to the original plan of whooping your ass."

Lord Kinoshita lets out a deep sigh. He snaps his finger in Kojo's direction. He senses a ball of fire forming before his very eyes. He leaps out of the way and pulls out his fishing rod. *Finally!* He rubs his hands together as the bob turns a bright orange. He hurls it in the direction of the Demon Lord. The villain flicks the bob down into the ground, where it is embedded in the floor.

Just then, several rocks begin to levitate. They have a silvery-white luster with a slight golden tinge about them. The larger ones rest closer to the ground, while the smaller ones propel into the ceiling. Booker leaps towards him. Kinoshita snaps his fingers in rapid succession, igniting fireballs right in front of Booker's face. He leaps back to avoid them.

Unfazed, the Demon Lord continues. "I see you're an electric user. We can work together, boy. I have mastered this element that serves as a great conductor. Many amateur alchemists believe this to be copper ore. But it's a new element: nickel. You are powering an electric current that also has a magnetic field. That's why these rocks float."

Kinoshita continues his barrage of attacks on Booker, with fireballs singeing the tips of his braids. He continues, "We can combine our skills to usher in the new industrial age. Faster boats. A way to store power. We can bring Japan to the forefront of innovation. You will have your place in my Empire."

Some of the rocks crack open, spilling brownish red magma onto the floor. Booker, unable to get in striking distance, unsheathes his sword and swings his blade continuously in place. The slashes create a propulsion of air waves that all target the Demon Lord. The foe dodges them, and the attacks land on the cave walls, which begin to crumple. A ripping echo reverberates throughout the space. It takes everything for Kojo to hear what Booker says.

"Kojo…focus the…aura…into yourself!"

Hearing this, Kojo jumps behind Booker. He closes his eyes and breathes deeply. He can sense the two men fighting in front of them but re-directs all his aura into himself. He stands alone in pitch blackness. A soft yellow tinge outlines his body, as his curly hair extends to form an afro.

He opens his eyes again, and now sees the blistering auras surrounding Booker and Lord Kinoshita. How much power and strength they both have, it's beyond impressive. *What power is this?*

Before doubt can enter his mind, Kojo feels another fireball forming in front of his face. Kojo prepares to dodge it; without prompting, he is teleported right behind his enemy. A roaring clap of thunder echoes throughout the cave. The Demon Lord turns around, with a new look on his face: shock. Booker grins harder than he ever has before.

"That right there is Impulse Speed, Kojo. A power only available to electrical users, or so I've been told. You're moving faster than your mind can process!" Booker exclaims.

The Demon Lord reaches out to grab Kojo, but he disappears in an instant. The boy reappears to the left of him. The Lord throws a flurry of attacks, engulfing his immediate surroundings in flames. But none of them hit Kojo, as he effortlessly dodges every movement even before he knows it's coming. A rapid series of shock waves hit the floating rocks.

Kojo appears in the air right above the Lord. He can barely look up before Kojo touches him in his temple. An electrical blast is released from his hands. The Demon Lord is thrown into the wall, unconscious. All the floating rocks tumble down to the floor. Kojo feels a dizziness come over him. He looks at Booker racing towards him, but his figure becomes increasingly blurry. A tremendous shock wave cripples the foundation of the cave. The ceiling falls toward them. Booker grabs Kojo and runs towards the exit. Kojo is unable to see anything but darkness in front of him. Even his senses can barely recognize the familiar pulse of the man holding him. The last thing he notices before passing out is the smell of acid and the sensation of wind washing across his face.

~~

A flock of turtle doves awaken Kojo to the new day. He blinks wearily to see the peach sky filled with baby blue clouds traveling lazily above him. *How long have I been out?* A damp towel covers his head. He looks to the left and sees a strange concoction in a bowl that smells of rosemary. Further back sit the trees, whistling a quiet tune on the riverbank. A stinging pain shoots through his head. He winces and rises up, but a firm hand grabs him by the shoulder and guides him back to rest.

"Relax."

Kojo looks at Booker, now brandishing a deep scar across his right eye.

"Booker...I...I'm so sorry I didn't know—*agh*-didn't know what would—"

"I told you to relax. Don't worry about all that."

Kojo heeds the counsel and lays in his temporary bed of straw. Booker continues rowing the boat upstream. With each stroke, a powerful swarm of bubbles follows behind them. As relaxed as Booker may appear, Kojo recognizes something rushed in his demeanor.

"So, you're the man of the hour, Kojo." Booker starts out. "Do you know what you were doing back at Mount Daisen? Use your head, don't talk."

Kojo strains to shake his head negatively.

"Yeah, I assumed as much. Well. Our friend The Demon Lord specialized in an element that conducts electricity extremely well. You provided enough electric power to sustain a village through the Dark Ages. But his metal wasn't in a pure enough state to carry that much charge. His impurities caused the rocks to crack, shooting electricity all over the place. It took everything I had to get you and escape."

Kojo looks at Booker, who reaches into the river and grabs a carp. He takes a bite out of it and places the carcass by his side. He notices Kojo's shocked face.

"I know, I know. Fish have high concentrations of the elements I need to heal and reforge my blade. You're not going to tell anyone, right?"

Kojo attempts to laugh at this but can only let out a series of coughs.

"I guess I could also eat beans, but I hate beans. Anyways, you've been fading in and out of consciousness for several days. But you're finally coming back around, and right on time."

Booker looks up to the waning moon. He takes some time before speaking.

"Most things in this life are corruptible, Kojo. Seeking this self-righteous purity of man only leads to division. It's a lesson Lord Kinoshita had to learn the hard way. Anything that requires others to be lesser than for the system to work is a bad system. The elements exist in harmony. Not in competition, and damn sure not in subjugation."

Booker places his hand on the boy's shoulder and continues. "My father told me something when I was younger: whenever I'm unsure of my decisions, look at the moon. That's where the only form of truth lies. Unreachable by men; incorruptible, yet always guiding us on the path we should take. Greatest advice I've ever been told."

Kojo looks up to see the moon. *Could anyone extend their aura to reach up there?* He feels the peaceful stream below him and decides to leave the question. For once, he's not in a rush to go anywhere. Booker brings the boat to rest at the riverbank. Kojo sees Efua sitting by the trees in her familiar kimono. She leaps up and runs towards them.

"And it hasn't failed yet."

AWaKen

STOries From THe OTHErSiDe